THE
QUIET
WOMAN

By the same author:

REMOTE CONTROL

DEATH TRAP

Harry Carmichael

THE QUIET WOMAN

Saturday Review Press
New York

Copyright © 1971 by Harry Carmichael
FIRST AMERICAN EDITION 1972

All rights reserved. No part of this work may be reproduced or transmitted in any form or by any means, electronic or mechanical, including photocopy, recording, or any information storage and retrieval system, without permission in writing from the publisher.

Library of Congress Catalog Number: 72-82843
ISBN 0-8415-0212-9

Saturday Review Press
230 Park Avenue
New York, New York 10017

PRINTED IN THE UNITED STATES OF AMERICA

. . . a horrid stillness first invades the ear,
And in that silence we the tempest fear.
　　　　　　　　John Dryden, 1631-1700

CHAPTER I

AT THREE O'CLOCK on the afternoon of Wednesday, November 4, a security van called at Lloyds Bank in Willesden to collect the Jauncey Engineering Company's payroll. By ten minutes past three the armoured truck had set off with two men locked inside to guard £53,600 in currency.

It took seven minutes to reach the North Circular Road, another two and a half minutes to arrive at the factory. As the driver turned into Bransby Lane he noted the time as usual. It was precisely twenty minutes past three when the big gates swung open and the van drove in. At three-twenty-one it pulled up outside the Administration building.

In another sixteen minutes the cash boxes had been carried into Wages Department, their contents checked, signed for and transferred to the office safe. At three-thirty-seven the security crew left.

The entry in the driver's log book recorded a routine cash delivery made without incident. There was no way he could have anticipated what would happen at the Jauncey Engineering works in three hours' time.

The factory worked overtime several nights a week but seldom on a Wednesday. Shortly after five p.m. on November 4, some eighteen hundred production workers had clocked out. By five past five, jostling crowds were streaming through the exit gates on Bransby Lane and the North Circular Road. Within a quarter of an hour the last stragglers had gone and only the office staff remained.

They left at five-thirty, except for a handful of executives and supervisors. By six o'clock the majority had gone. Minutes later only two offices still had their lights on.

Reg Tugwell completed his first hourly tour of the works just after six. When he returned to the Patrol Office inside

Bransby Lane gates he told Alfie Platt, 'Some people have no homes to go to. Head cashier says he doesn't know when he'll be finished and Mrs Marshall in Wages is still at it.'

Alfie said, 'If they did more work during the day and drank less tea they might finish same time as everybody else.'

'You can say that again. Are those all the clock cards?'

'Every single one. Now I'll be off. Weather forecast says it'll be wet and windy during the night.'

'I heard it,' Reg said. 'Won't bother me as much as Vic. The rain isn't expected to be heavy until the early hours. With a bit of luck I'll be snug in bed by then. If you see Vic Ryan tell him not to be late.'

'I'll do that,' Alfie said.

Tugwell walked with him to the gates, locked up after he had gone and returned to the Patrol Office. In the record book, he noted: *Day patrolman left* 6.10. *Mr Graham and Mrs Marshall working late. All exits secured. Main factory lights switched off. Everything OK.*

It was raining heavily and blowing half a gale when Vic Ryan reached the factory. The time was then a few minutes before one a.m. From Bransby Lane he could see there were no lights showing in the Patrol Office.

The other buildings also were in darkness. Throughout the whole length of Centre Way—the main road which bisected the factory—nothing stirred. All he could hear was the wind and the gurgle of water in the gutters.

With his back to the driving rain he waited patiently outside the gates. It was barely five minutes to one. Reg would be along pretty soon. He always pinched some time off the last patrol of his shift. On a night like this he would be only too anxious to get off home.

Ryan huddled in his oilskins and watched the road which branched left and ran past Admin. Any minute now he would see Reg's bobbing flashlamp. Every tour of the works was completed by passing the Administration block and then crossing Centre Way to the Patrol Office. Any minute now . . . and the sooner the better.

But the minutes went by without any sign of Reg Tugwell. At five past one Ryan was in no mood to wait any longer.

It had been months since anyone had rung the bell late at night and the clamour was startling. He took his finger off the button and listened. He could still hear nothing but the noise of the rain and the buffeting wind.

By then he had an uneasy feeling that something was wrong—very far wrong. This had never happened before. Reg must have been taken ill on one of his rounds . . . or had an accident . . .

That was when Ryan discovered the gates were unlocked. The right half moved as he leaned against it to peer along the streaming darkness of Centre Way.

He pushed it open just enough to let him through. With the wind and the rain beating in his face he hurried to the Patrol Office.

It was locked. He had known it was bound to be locked.

Reg Tugwell had gone on his rounds—and not come back. He might be anywhere.

To search the factory, building by building, would take an hour or more. There were so many places to look.

Ryan told himself he would get no thanks for setting about the task on his own. The longer he spent hunting for Reg the more time he would waste. He had to get help.

If Reg was all right he would have heard the bell. It was loud enough to be heard the length and breadth of the factory.

Whatever had happened to him, the gates should never have been left unsecured. Anybody could have got in . . . and out again. They might be getting farther away every second.

Nothing could explain the unlocked gates—neither illness nor accident. Reg knew the rules. He knew that carelessness could cost him his job.

So something must be wrong. Reg was in trouble—bad trouble. Danger lurked in the blustering darkness. Vic could feel it all around him—an atmosphere of menace that seemed to be drawing closer every moment. Fear laid a cold hand on him as he stood in the doorway of the Patrol Office.

There was only one thing to be done. And he must do it soon.

This was police business. They would know what to do. If Reg was anywhere in the factory they would find him . . . dead or alive.

That unwelcome thought goaded Ryan into action. He left the shelter of the doorway and trudged, head down to the wind, past the adjoining stores block and on to the open area where a new production building was in process of construction.

Piles of bricks and rubble, skeleton girders, a concrete-mixer—all loomed black against the yellow glow of street lamps on the North Circular Road. When he stepped off the secure footing of Centre Way he stumbled into a wheelbarrow and almost fell over the edge of an excavation where part of a new road ended.

The ground was slippery and pitted with water-filled holes. He splashed from one to the other, groping here and there, until he found something that felt like half a brick. Then he made his way back to the Patrol Office.

A couple of blows smashed the window. When he had chipped away the remaining fragments of glass he climbed inside and put on the light.

His hands were muddy, his fingers numb with cold. The first time he dialled the emergency call he was clumsy and stumbled over one of the digits. Before he tried again he wiped his hands on a rag and gave them a brisk rub to get his circulation going. Then slowly and carefully he dialled the number once more . . .

The desk sergeant listened, asked one or two questions and promised he would have a police car at the factory within minutes. He gave the patrolman renewed confidence.

'. . . You stay right where you are, Mr Ryan. If you've got intruders on the premises we'll send in a couple of dogs to flush 'em out.'

The first car arrived at one-twelve. Two other vehicles were outside the gates by one-fifteen. They cordoned off both Bransby Lane and the North Circular Road entrances and then split up into separate groups, two of them each with a dog-handler.

Headlamps lit the entire length of Centre Way from Bransby Lane to the car park beyond the Foundry as the various groups began their search. By then the wind had slackened and it was raining steadily.

A-group proceeded to the far end of Centre Way and took up a position where they could see the whole of the factory: B-group criss-crossed from building to building, checking the entrances and exits of the production shops: C-group—two officers accompanied by Vic Ryan inspected Stores and then turned their attention to the Admin block.

That was where the search ended. As Ryan used his key on the door, he halted and said, 'Did you hear a noise like someone banging? It's gone now but I was sure ... there it is again.'

They all heard it—a rhythmic drumming sound that started and stopped half a dozen times. Then everything was still except for the hissing of the rain.

Vic Ryan said, 'I think I know where it's coming from. Hold on a second.'

He went inside and the beam of his flashlamp picked out a switch on the wall. A moment later the corridor lights came on.

With Ryan leading the way they took the second passage on the left, turned right and then left again. On a door at the end a notice read: WAGES DEPARTMENT—No Admittance.

Only a couple of lights burned in the long room with its three rows of tidy desks. An inner door had a plaque: Mrs Marshall—Private.

No lights were on in the glass-walled private office. The door was open.

One of the policemen said, 'You better keep behind us, Mr Ryan. Never know what we'll bump into.'

At the sound of his voice there was scuffling in the inner

room and a muffled noise like someone in pain. The rhythmic drumming began again.

When they got to the open door everything went quiet. All that Ryan could hear was the threshing of rain on the roof. Then the other policeman reached inside and switched on the light.

Over the officer's shoulder Ryan saw a man lying on the floor. He was bound hand and foot with adhesive tape round his ankles and wrists. Several lengths tied his feet to one of the heating pipes under the window. A strip of plaster had been stuck over his mouth.

Ryan said, 'Well, I'll be damned! It's Reg Tugwell. Wonder how long he's been tied up like that?'

They freed his arms and legs and helped him into a chair. One of the policemen said, 'This might hurt a bit—but it's the only way.'

He pried loose a corner of the tape covering Tugwell's mouth. With a quick pull he ripped it off.

Reg cried out and clapped both hands to his face. With his eyes screwed up tight, he wailed, 'Bloody hell! What did you want to do that for? Haven't I gone through enough already? What a night I've had! What a bloody night . . .'

Somebody brought him a glass of water. Then they massaged his limbs until he told them to leave him alone.

'. . . I'm all right now. If it wasn't for my head I'd be OK.'

'What's wrong with your head?'

'I've got a lump on it like an egg where the bastard hit me—that's what's wrong.'

He put a hand to his head just above and behind his left ear. He grumbled, 'Wouldn't be surprised if I've got a cracked skull.'

'Did you see who it was?'

Tugwell took another sip of water. In a stronger voice, he said, 'Of course I saw him . . . just before he hit me. Mister bloody Graham, that's who it was.'

'Who's Mr Graham?'

'The head cashier. He was hiding behind the door and

she—' Tugwell pointed to a spot in front of the twin-lock safe built into the wall—'she was standing there looking scared to death. I heard something close beside me and I tried to get out of the way but I was too slow.'

He felt again and grimaced with pain. Then he went on, 'I just managed to catch a glimpse of Graham. He had a shiny thing in his hand and he brought it down smack on my head . . . and that's the last I knew until I woke up lying on the floor.'

'You're sure it was Graham who struck you?'

'I'm absolutely positive.'

'What about this woman you saw? Did you recognize her?'

'Yes . . . same as I recognized him. It was Mrs Marshall, the wages supervisor. And that reminds me . . .'

Tugwell stood up. On unsteady feet he walked two or three steps towards the safe.

In a tone of bewilderment, he said, 'It was open . . . and there was bundles of money on the desk . . . and two cases packed with notes and . . . oh, bloody hell.'

He went forward another step and reached out to take hold of the handle of the safe. He seemed reluctant to go too near.

One of the policemen said, 'Don't touch it. They'll want to test for fingerprints. Just you sit down and relax.'

As he turned to the door, he added, 'You're going to have a lot of talking to do before the night's over.'

CHAPTER II

THURSDAY MORNING, November 5, Detective-Superintendent Tom Hennant got to the office at eight-thirty. An hour later he had a phone call from the Assistant Commissioner.

'. . . I want you to take charge of the inquiries, Tom. Judging by what Willesden have managed to piece together it looks straightforward enough . . . but let me know what you think.'

'Yes, certainly. I'll get on with it—' Hennant looked at his cluttered desk and sighed—'right away, sir.'

The AC said, 'Good. Willesden have already circulated descriptions of Graham and Mrs Marshall.'

'Who had time to go to ground before the theft was discovered,' Hennant said.

'Well, they haven't been seen since the factory patrolman was given a nasty headache.'

'Is this fellow Graham married, sir?'

'Yes. Lives with his wife at Crouch End.'

'Until last night,' Hennant said. 'Wasn't she worried when he didn't return home?'

'Not until it got very late. Seemingly she was just about to phone the police when a local inspector called at her house in Maryland Avenue.'

'How about the woman—the Wages Department supervisor? Is there a Mr Marshall?'

'Oh, yes. He was at home all yesterday nursing a dose of flu. Never guessed, of course, what his wife was up to.'

'Husbands rarely do,' Hennant said. 'Often wonder whether it's misplaced trust or plain masculine vanity.'

'Probably a combination of both. However, to get back to this case, it seems she told Marshall she'd be working overtime and he wasn't to expect her till pretty late.'

'That's all very well, sir. But didn't he think he ought to do something when it got to one a.m. and she still wasn't home?'

'Probably would've done. But he took a hot toddy with some aspirins about nine o'clock and slept like a log from then until somebody from the station at Dollis Hill got him out of bed. Nearly roused the neighbourhood to do it, too.'

The AC added, 'I've sent you the file. It's all there . . . but if you have any questions have a word with Chief Inspector Edmund at Willesden. And keep me posted.'

Superintendent Hennant said, 'Of course, sir. I'll let you

know soon as there are any developments.'

He read through the folder quickly, made a précis of the events at Jauncey Engineering Company's works and then studied each document in careful detail. From time to time he made marginal comments. Finally he checked all the known facts and listed them in the form of a time-table.

The main report included biographical remarks on the missing personnel. Hennant re-read this section with special interest.

>HAROLD VICTOR GRAHAM : Age 45 : Married : No children : B.Econ. London Univ : Worked for mail-order company until he joined Jauncey Engineering nine years ago as manager Accounts Dept. Later promoted to Head Cashier.
>Enjoyed complete trust of Jauncey's board of directors. Works manager insists there must be some alternative explanation for Graham's disappearance. He was known to the company's executives as a man of absolute integrity.

Under his breath, Superintendent Hennant murmured, 'Shows how people can be mistaken—an expensive mistake, at that.'

>YVONNE MARSHALL : Age 30 : Married : Had one child who was killed in road accident returning from school : Worked for Jauncey Engineering before marriage : Re-employed by Company after death of child.
>Handled considerable sums of money over many years. Never any suspicion that she was not entirely trustworthy.

Then there was a footnote. The superintendent talked to himself again as he read it.

Two keys were required to unlock the safe. One has

always been in the possession of Harold Graham; the other was entrusted to Mrs Marshall. Theft of the payroll would have been impossible without collusion between these two employees.

Inquiries at their respective homes reveal that no photographs of them can be found although in both cases wedding pictures, holiday snaps, etc. are known to have existed. It would seem obvious that Graham and Marshall removed all such photographs recently.

The following descriptions have been circulated to all stations.

On the instructions of AC Godolphin copies are also being sent to Interpol.

The listed physical characteristics of the wanted couple were obtained from Graham's wife and Mrs Marshall's husband. They were checked with business colleagues who knew them well.

Harold Victor Graham: Height 5 ft. 8 ins.: spare build: erect carriage: dark hair greying at temples: brown eyes: thin mouth: square chin with cleft: good teeth: fair complexion: no distinguishing marks.

This man is 45 years of age but looks younger. Has an educated voice and speaks slowly. No particular accent. Can converse in French and Italian.

Yvonne Marshall: Height 5 ft. 5 ins.: slim build and good figure: brunette with grey eyes, naturally brown hair, attractive features.

She is 30 years of age. Speaks well. Slight north-country accent. Is described as a woman of poise and charm.

Superintendent Hennant walked to the window and stared down absently at the plane trees on the Embankment while he painted mental pictures. Then he came back to his desk, scrawled a comment on the memo pad and read it aloud.

'Personable man of maturity and education ... good-looking woman, fifteen years his junior. He had one key to the safe, she had the other. And the safe contained over fifty thousand pounds in used, unmarked notes. Anybody would call that a real merger of interests—financial and physical.'

The next page dealt with the interrogation of Reg Tugwell, factory patrolman on the evening shift. Hennant read it again with even closer attention.

> Jauncey Engineering operates a 3-shift system of patrols at the factory: 5.00 p.m. to 1.00 a.m.: 1.00 a.m. to 9.00 a.m.: 9.00 a.m. to 5.00 p.m. Tugwell was on the evening shift.
> He took over from Alf Platt, day-shift man, at five o'clock. Platt stayed on until six p.m. to collect the works' clock cards.
> It is routine procedure for the cards to be handed in to Wages Department by the day patrolman making his first round of the factory at nine o'clock Thursday morning. Wages are paid out on Friday.
> Keys to the factory gates are kept in the Patrol Office, which is always locked while the man on duty is making his rounds. To obtain the key to the gates at Bransby Lane it was necessary to relieve Tugwell of the key to the office.
> He states that he was on his second patrol when it began raining heavily. That would be about 6.45 p.m. He was then proceeding along the return route which passes the rear of the Foundry, the principal Machine Shop and the Administration building.
> Instead of completing his patrol he decided to return for his oilskins. So he gave the M/c Shop and Admin only a cursory inspection as he trotted towards First Avenue—a side road running past the entrance to Admin and coming out almost opposite the Patrol Office.
> While he was still some distance from the Admin building he could see two cars parked at the entrance. At about the same time he saw a woman coming out of the doorway.
> The spread of light from inside did not reach very far but he says she was carrying what seemed to be an attaché case in each hand. In spite of poor visibility Tugwell is certain that the woman was Mrs Marshall.

Her behaviour aroused his suspicions. When she caught sight of him she darted between the two cars and, for a few seconds, he was unable to see what she was doing. However, he did hear a noise like the slamming of a boot-lid.

Almost immediately the woman rushed back into Admin. Now she had nothing in her hands. As she ran inside the building he heard her calling to somebody.

Before he followed her he took a hasty look in the boot of the leading car. On the floor he saw half a dozen cases similar to those she had been carrying. Two of them had been tossed carelessly into the boot: the others were in a neat double stack.

He closed the lid and ran into Admin. Everything was silent. The lights were on in the main corridor and one of the side passages but he could see no sign of Mrs Marshall.

When he got to the Wages Department the place was in darkness. At the far end the light was on in Mrs Marshall's private room.

He is not sure if the door was shut or partly open.

He remembers that he went in without knocking. As soon as he was inside he saw Mrs Marshall. She had both hands covering her mouth and her eyes were very frightened.

There were two attaché cases on the desk, both of them filled with bundles of money. Other bundles lay nearby.

That was all he had time to see before someone came from behind the door. Tugwell had a momentary glimpse of a man with one arm upraised. In his hand he held a round semi-transparent object which glistened in the light.

The man was Harold Graham, head cashier of the company. Of this, Tugwell has no doubt. He is prepared to swear to the identification if, and when, called upon to do so.

He states that he tried to throw himself out of the way but he was too late. The shining round object struck him on the side of the head and he remembers no more.

He cannot say how long he was unconscious. When he

awoke he found himself in darkness. His head hurt badly and he was unable to move.

After a while he realized his arms and legs were bound with some kind of tape. A strip of plaster stuck over his mouth prevented him calling for help.

It was an unnecessary precaution. Bransby Lane is little used at night and the Wages Department is too far from the North Circular Road. In any case, the noise of passing traffic made it unlikely that anyone would have heard him.

When the bell rang outside the Patrol Office he knew it must be time for change of shift. From then on he tried to attract attention by banging his heels on the floor. It was this noise which eventually led to his release.

Tugwell was examined by a police doctor who found considerable swelling on the side of the head. He was taken to Neasden Hospital and X-rayed. There was no sign of a skull fracture but the casualty officer decided to detain him overnight in case he was suffering from concussion.

A check of the safe in Yvonne Marshall's room revealed that the delivery made by the security firm at 3.25 p.m. yesterday afternoon was missing. £53,000 in notes had gone and only £1,000 in silver and nickel remained.

The stolen money consisted of £33,000 in bundles of 100 £1 notes : £20,000 in bundles of 100 £5 notes—all used and not marked in any way. Also stolen was a float of between £400 and £600 normally kept in the safe.

If Tugwell's recollection can be relied on the cash was taken away in eight attaché cases, each measuring approximately 18 ins. by 12 ins. by 2 ins. to 3 ins. in depth. Based on the capacity required—as shown on the appended list obtained from Lloyds Bank—it would seem that his estimate of size is roughly correct, assuming these figures to be inside measurements.

The list from the bank showed approximate sizes and weights of the notes in bundles of 100, each fastened with a paper band. Superintendent Hennant did some calculations, drew a rectangular diagram on his memo pad and checked it against the patrolman's statement.

A bundle of 100 £1 notes was slightly less than 6 ins. long and 3 ins. wide. As near as made no difference it was $\frac{1}{2}$ in. thick; weight three and one-fifth ounces. Comparable figures for a bundle of 100 £5 notes were: $5\frac{1}{2}$ ins. by $3\frac{1}{2}$ ins. by $\frac{1}{2}$ in.: weight three and one-third ounces.

Hennant filled in his diagram to represent a case measuring 18 ins. by 12 ins. by 2 ins. Given that these were inside dimensions, the case would hold 48 bundles in stacks of 4. There was room for two rows each of six stacks: total value of contents—£4,800.

Seven cases would amount to £33,600. Similarly, one more case could have accommodated the missing £20,000 in £5 notes. If there had been a float of at least £400 in the safe, then the figures balanced.

So Reg Tugwell's recollection had been correct. There had been eight cases—six in the boot of the car and two on Mrs Marshall's desk.

The superintendent pictured in his mind the woman whom Tugwell saw coming out of Admin. He said she was carrying two cases.

That was feasible as well. Each case would weigh nine or ten pounds, allowing for the weight of the case itself. She could have carried two of them.

Hennant murmured to himself '. . . Nicely organized. Graham probably had the attaché cases made to his own specification. He packed them with bundles of notes and she took them outside, two at a time, and loaded them into the boot of the car . . .'

The next thought followed logically. If Tugwell had not reached the Admin block earlier than scheduled, Graham and Mrs Marshall would have completed their task before he got back to the Patrol Office. All they had to do then was to wait for him to return so that he could open the Bransby Lane gates to let them out.

Superintendent Hennant scribbled through the diagram on his memo pad. He knew nearly the whole story now. The rest was provided by the fingerprint report.

On the handle and the edge of the safe door, prints had been found overlying others that were smudged and unidentifiable. The more recent prints matched those on articles known to have been handled by Harold Graham.

One of the articles was a paperweight in the shape of a sea-urchin made of solid glass with a milky interior design. It weighed almost two pounds.

Reg Tugwell said it looked like the shiny object he had seen in Graham's hand just before the cashier struck him. There was nothing else of a similar nature in the office.

A paragraph at the end of the file mentioned that a part-used reel of zinc oxide plaster had been found under Mrs Marshall's desk. It was the same type as the plaster used to tie up the patrolman. Inquiries revealed that it had come from the first-aid cabinet in Wages Department.

Superintendent Hennant got up and walked to the window again and stood for a while watching a tug beating its way up river against the drag of the outgoing tide. Beneath a sullen sky the trees down below strained in the wind.

He wondered how long Graham and Yvonne Marshall had been planning to rob their employers and which of them had first thought of the idea. More often than not it was the woman.

Women had the capacity to be both romantic and practical. Their hearts might lead them into folly but their heads never lost sight of ways and means.

Mrs Marshall would be no different. She sounded like the kind of woman who could inspire any man to cast off his humdrum everyday existence.

It was a straightforward case. Everything fitted—motive, opportunity, the commission of the crime. At seven o'clock on the evening of Wednesday, November 4, a man and his mistress had gone off to start a new life with £53,000 of stolen money.

Under his breath, Superintendent Hennant said, 'Now all we have to do is find them.'

CHAPTER III

SOMEBODY HAD STUCK A NOTE in the platen of Quinn's typewriter: *There was a phone message for you at ten a.m. Since you were not here, Features took it. If you want to know who, what and why, ask them. PS. Why don't you get up earlier in the morning?*

He read the note without interest and then looked up at the office clock. Five past ten . . . just five minutes late. He was never supposed to be there before ten. The way he felt they were lucky he had got there at all.

. . . *Must be true that boredom makes you need more sleep. Nine hours should be enough. Can't say I didn't sleep well. Always do when I've had a skinful . . .*

It was the sameness of his leisure time that got him down. Always the same people making the same comments about the same things, repeating the same threadbare anecdotes . . . ad infinitum, ad nauseam. Never an original thought or any real wit.

. . . *You've got a sour stomach, that's your trouble. You should have a couple of early nights and go to bed with a hot drink of that stuff they advertise on the telly. Makes you get up next morning frantic to milk the cows and clean out the hen-house . . .*

There was always someone phoning him. Pity was it seldom led to anything. Must have been a crackpot who coined the phrase: No news is good news. He would have known better if he had earned his living on a paper.

The minute-hand of the clock moved on to ten past ten. Quinn yawned and stretched and asked himself why it was that he always liked the idea of doing nothing except when he had nothing to do. Must be psychological. Everything was psychological these days.

He rubbed the ache in his neck while he read the note again and wondered who had phoned at ten o'clock and why anyone should expect him to be at the office so early. Then he went upstairs to the canteen and had a cup of strong tea to wash the taste out of his mouth.

The need for a cigarette was like palpitation somewhere inside. He searched his pockets and found he had none. If he bought a packet he would smoke too many too soon. One was all he wanted . . . one at a time.

The man in Features said, 'Tell you what. I'll give you my address.'

'Do you mean you've left your cigarettes at home?'

'No. But if you know where I live you can bring your bed and I'll keep you.'

'Highly comical,' Quinn said. 'Is that how you treat an old friend?'

'Old—yes, friend—no. It's the treat part that I object to. Anyway, I've given it up.'

'Mean you've stopped smoking?'

'No, I've just stopped acting Santa Claus. For your information, there's a shop down the street with so many cigarettes they're selling them.'

Quinn said, 'You must've been twins. You're too funny for one. Can't you see I've got second-stage withdrawal symptoms?'

The man in Features sighed. Then he rummaged among the papers on his desk until he found a flattened cigarette-packet.

He said, 'OK. Here you are. I'd have you know it's my last.'

'Really? You'll have to buy some more. Got a light?'

'That, too. Seems all you've got is a strong inclination. Bring the equipment next time and I'll give you a blood transfusion. The way you look you could do with one. Last time I saw a fellow the colour you are right now he'd been dead three days.'

'That's just how I feel,' Quinn said.

He lit the cigarette, inhaled deeply and began to cough. The spasm lasted until he was breathless.

The man in Features said, 'Ah, that's a lot better. Now you've got nice rosy cheeks. Don't think bloodshot eyes are an improvement though. You should wear dark glasses.'

When he got his breath back, Quinn said, 'I won't tell you what you should do. It's anatomically impossible. Now what's this phone message you've got for me?'

'Message? Oh, yes. Well, some bloke called Begley wanted to speak to you. Says you know him.'

'By name only. He gives me bits of information once in a while. What's he got this time?'

'A vague sort of tip if you ask me. Seems he has a pal who works for Jauncey Engineering on the North Circular Road. This pal told Begley there's been fun and games at the factory during the night—police and dogs and lots of excitement. Doesn't know what's actually happened because it's all very hush-hush but he's convinced it must be something big.'

Quinn said, 'Does he? Maybe things are looking up at last . . .'

The press officer at New Scotland Yard made no secret of what had taken place. '. . . I've just prepared a release for the newspapers. As you'll appreciate, we need all the co-operation and publicity we can get. The wider we spread their descriptions around, the quicker we may get results.'

'What about the two cars the patrolman saw?'

'No trace of them. One belonged to Graham and we've circulated its registration number but we've no knowledge of the other one.'

'Hasn't Mrs Marshall or her husband got a car?'

'Yes . . . well, it would be more correct to say his firm provides him with one—an Austin 1300. But it couldn't have been his car that was used last night. It was being serviced. Mrs Marshall took it into the garage in Dollis Hill yesterday morning.'

'And it's been there ever since?'

'Definitely. She was supposed to collect it on her way home but—'

'—but she had bigger fish to fry,' Quinn said. 'I'm surprised she even bothered to take it to the garage.'

'Her husband asked her to do it for him. He's got flu and

spent yesterday in bed.'

'So she couldn't have picked a better time to forsake hearth, home and hubby. What does he do for a living?'

'He's a rep with a firm of roofing contractors. Travels all over the country.'

Quinn said, 'But not with fifty-four thousand pounds in the boot of his car. How does he like being left to cuddle a hot-water bottle while his wife's cuddling Harold Graham, lately departed?'

'Same as you'd like it, I suppose.'

'Never suspected there was any monkey-business bettween her and the cashier?'

'Didn't have the slightest idea. Detective-Superintendent Hennant who interviewed him says the man was in a daze.'

The phone crackled and jumbled voices broke in on the line. Then the press officer asked, 'Anything else you want to know?'

'Yes . . . two things to be going on with. If Mrs Marshall wasn't using her husband's car—'

'She wasn't . . . that's for sure. It never left the garage from the moment she handed over the ignition key. Incidentally, while the car was being serviced another vehicle backed into it and made a mess of the whole front end. It'll take another couple of days to repair.'

Quinn said, 'This certainly isn't Marshall's lucky week.'

'Oh, I don't know. The car belongs to his firm, and in any case it's insured.'

'Pity he didn't take out insurance against the loss of his wife.'

'He's better off without her,' the press officer said. 'I wouldn't fancy being married to a woman like that.'

'Judging by her description she might not fancy being married to a man like you.'

'Probably not. Now how about going about your business and leaving me to get on with mine?'

'Soon,' Quinn said. 'If Graham left the factory in his own car, whose car was Mrs Marshall driving? That's what I'd like to know.'

'So would we. Finished?'

'One last question.'

'Well?'

'A man and a woman can lie low almost indefinitely if they've made their arrangements well in advance. But how do you make two cars disappear?'

'If we knew that, we might have some idea where Graham and his lady-love went when they drove out of the factory . . . and we haven't. Or didn't I make that clear at the outset?'

'Don't get testy,' Quinn said. 'I suppose Jauncey Engineering are covered for theft of cash stolen from their safe?'

'I'd imagine so. But this isn't ordinary theft. The safe was opened with keys that had been given to a pair of trusted employees. Whether the insurance pays out in these circumstances is something I wouldn't know.'

Quinn said, 'Neither would I. But I've got a very knowledgeable friend.'

'That's a contradiction in terms. If he were really knowledgeable—' the press officer's voice receded from the phone —'he couldn't be a friend of yours.'

'Remind me next time we meet that we're not speaking,' Quinn said. 'I'm not taking that from anyone . . . as the actress said to the bishop . . . '

John Piper's number was engaged. It was still engaged when Quinn tried again at a quarter to eleven.

He paid a second visit to the canteen and had another cup of tea. Then he went to the washroom.

After he had splashed cold water in his face he stood looking at himself in the mirror with distaste. His reflection seemed equally repelled.

The man in Features had been right—his eyes were bloodshot. There was nothing pleasing, either, about thin features, a pasty skin, hair the colour of damp straw. A scratch on the side of his chin where he had cut himself while shaving didn't improve his looks.

. . . That was all you were short of. In olden times they used to advise a pregnant woman to look the other way when someone like you went by . . . Bet your mother got a

helluva shock when she woke up and found you beside her . . .

He combed his hair, unfastened his stringy tie and made a fresh knot. It helped a little—but only a little. He told himself he still looked like one of Frankenstein's early experiments.

It was eleven o'clock when he went back to Editorial and rang Piper's office once again. This time he got through.

Piper said, 'Nice to hear from you. How's life?'

'I wouldn't know. I've opted out. The way things are going I'm tempted to join a monastery.'

'One of those days, is it?'

'Yes, you might say I'm feeling sorry for myself.'

'Any special reason?'

'No, just me. I got out of bed on the wrong side this morning. You all right?'

'Fine, thanks.'

Quinn said, 'Good.'

He wanted to ask about Jane but it might sound as if he were fishing for an invitation. And the last time the three of them had spent an evening together it had not proved very successful.

When a man married he moved into a sphere where there was no room for the friends of his bachelor days. They were bound to drift apart. It was no use fighting against the inevitable, no fun being odd man out.

Piper asked, 'How about having lunch with me?'

At the back of Quinn's mind a little voice complained *'. . . That's his conscience speaking. Not that I can see why he should feel guilty. I'd hate to think he felt sorry for me. Let him live his own life and I'll live mine. Damned if I'm going to get wed just so's we can make up a foursome . . .'*

'Not today,' Quinn said. 'Thanks all the same but I'm on a job of work. Actually, that's why I phoned you. I've got a query about insurance and I thought you'd know the answer.'

'I'll do my best,' Piper said.

He listened to a condensed account of what had happened at the Jauncey Engineering works the previous night.

Then he said, 'You're asking me whether the firm is covered or not and I'm afraid I can't give you an answer off the cuff.'

'Too bad,' Quinn said. 'You disappoint me.'

'Sorry about that . . . but it's a bit tricky.'

'Why?'

'Well, the usual insurance against theft excludes cash stolen where collusion has taken place.'

'Always?'

'No. The limiting clause can be deleted—used to be allowed without any increase in premium but not any longer —and I couldn't give you a proper answer in this case unless I checked the policy.'

'So Jauncey Engineering could be left holding a fifty-four-thousand-pound baby?'

'Perhaps. As I say, it all depends. You'll have to give me notice of that question.'

'Take all the time you want. No hurry.'

'Any idea who the insurers are?'

'Not a clue. If you like, you could ask someone in authority at the works.'

Piper said, 'I don't like. They'd tell me to mind my own business.'

'It is your business. You're an insurance assessor, aren't you?'

'Oh, yes. But I don't interest myself in this sort of affair unless I'm employed to do so.'

'All right. Why not approach Jauncey Engineering Company or their insurance people and offer your services?'

'Because I don't tout for trade,' Piper said.

Quinn whistled the opening bars of 'Mad Dogs and Englishmen'. Then he said, 'You make it sound like prostitution. But never mind. I suppose there'll be a reward for information leading to de-da . . . de-da . . . de-da . . . eh?'

'Bound to be.'

'How much would you think?'

'The usual ten per cent, I'd say.'

'M-m-m . . . five thousand quid. That'll get a few shady characters sniffing around.'

'They wouldn't know where to start,' Piper said. 'Graham and Mrs Marshall are one-shot amateurs: no form, no *modus operandi,* no criminal associates.'

Quinn said, 'And no photographs. The newspapers will be given only an artist's impression of what the runaway couple look like. This reminds me of the start of a race to stake out your claim on a goldfield.'

'What are you talking about?'

'Everybody's got an equal chance. Anyone can strike lucky . . . same as with Premium Bonds. The police are starting from scratch like all the rest of us.'

'Are you being serious . . . for a change?'

'Unfortunately, no. But—' Quinn had a brief spasm of coughing—'but I could sure use that reward money.'

He cleared his throat and added, 'Somebody knows where the love-birds are right now . . . but doesn't realize it.'

Piper said, 'All you have to do is find the somebody. I wish you the best of luck.'

'Sarcasm doesn't deter me,' Quinn said. 'You might get a big surprise . . . although I don't think so.'

The editorial morning conference lasted longer than usual. It was almost twelve before he managed to have a word with the news editor.

'. . . I feel it's the kind of story that has real possibilities. If you turn me loose on it—'

'You'd proceed to get pickled,' the news editor said. 'Do you imagine I came up the Thames in a bathtub? Instead of turning you loose I'd rather turn you out. Now that's a much better idea.'

'But—'

'No buts. If you do work on this story there's going to be no repetition of the Vanishing Quinn act we've had far too often. You keep me in the picture each day and every day. Understand?'

Quinn said, 'Yes, sir. Very good, sir. Three bags full, sir. Was there anything else?'

'Yes. You need a haircut. Good morning.'

CHAPTER IV

Brinton Drive lay on the left of Dollis Hill Lane—a winding road of suburban houses, each with its privet hedge and small front lawn and a leaded coloured-glass panel in the door. There was also coloured glass in the top part of the bay windows.

Unlike its immediate neighbours, No. 19 had wrought-iron gates. The houses on either side had a wooden or asbestos garage: No. 19 had a brick-built structure which looked comparatively new. Quinn had the thought that the Marshall home showed the advantage of two incomes.

. . . But now there'll only be one. Her husband's suffered a double loss. Even if he re-marries, his second wife may not want to go out to work. He'll have to sue for divorce on grounds of desertion. No proof of adultery unless it can be proved they're living together . . . which is only conjecture until the police catch up with them . . . if the police ever catch up with them . . .

As he walked up the path he could see into the ground-floor room. It had too much furniture. Quinn's second thought was that the Marshalls had not had anything else to spend their money on.

. . . Maybe the loss of the child had an adverse effect on their marriage. Could have made a change in her attitude towards her husband. Home to her wouldn't be a home any longer. Might even be that she had to blame somebody for what had happened and so she blamed him. Irrational . . . but when a woman's badly hurt she doesn't employ logic . . .

He touched the bellpush lightly. Somewhere behind a closed door a flat-toned bell rang. Then there was no sound of any kind.

While he waited he asked himself why he should be making allowances for Mrs Marshall. Betrayal of trust . . . conspiracy . . . the theft of a large sum of money . . .

If ever she stood in the dock no jury would accept that there had been extenuating circumstances. But first they had to catch her . . .

Quinn pressed the bellpush again. As he took his finger off the button he heard footsteps coming down the stairs. Then the door opened.

He was a broad-shouldered man with deep-set eyes and heavy features. Judging by his expression he was in no mood to receive visitors.

In a clipped voice, he said, 'I heard you the first time but I hoped you'd go away. What do you want?'

'If you're Mr Marshall—'

'Who did you think I was? This is No. 19 Brinton Drive, isn't it?'

'Yes, but there's no harm in—'

'Skip it. I've had enough talk for one day. Besides, you're too late. He's gone.'

'Who's gone?'

'Your boss—Superintendent Hennant. So far as I know he's on his way back to Scotland Yard. If you're interested—'

'I'm not,' Quinn said. 'Hennant isn't my boss. I don't belong to the police.'

Marshall rested his shoulder against the leading edge of the door and made a pointed mouth. He asked, 'Then who are you?'

'My name's Quinn. I'm from the *Morning Post*.'

'Oh, a reporter.'

'Well, you could call me that.'

'I could call you lots of things. Why pester me? If you want to know what's happened, ask the police.'

'They've already told me what's happened,' Quinn said. 'Your wife and the head cashier of Jauncey Engineering have gone off and so has fifty-four thousand pounds of the company's money. But those are only the bare bones. I'd like to put some flesh on them . . . if you'll help me.'

'Why should I? The whole affair makes me sick. I don't want to discuss it any more. I'm going to have enough damned notoriety without inviting it.'

'That's a foregone conclusion,' Quinn said. 'I came here because I thought you might like to get some of your own back.'

Marshall straightened himself. With less aggression in his voice, he asked, 'Just what does that mean?'

'No more and no less than it says. Your wife and this fellow Graham have done the dirty on you properly. Wouldn't you like to see them stuck away?'

'Of course I would. But what can I do? I've already told the police all I know—and that wasn't very much.'

He drew back a step. After a moment's hesitation, he said, 'You'd better come inside. I don't know what it'll achieve . . . but you can have five minutes.'

When Quinn went past him he shut the door and led the way into the over-furnished room. Then he said, 'The whole world's upside down today. They got me out of bed about two a.m. and I never slept a wink after that. I didn't believe it at first but after what Superintendent Hennant had to say it all began to make a pattern . . . a lousy, stinking pattern.'

He sat down and let his hands droop between his knees. With a look of doubt, he added, I don't think I really care what happens to my wife and that man Graham. What difference will it make to me? I'm finished. My whole life's been destroyed . . . and all inside a few hours.'

Quinn said, 'I'm sorry. I can understand how you feel. But in time you'll get over it. This sort of thing has happened to other husbands and they just had to pick up the pieces and start again.'

'Easier said than done. If I'd only suspected what was going on. Right under my very nose . . .'

'It's always the case,' Quinn said.

'So they say. But it always happens to somebody else. Now—' he massaged his knees and sighed—'now it's me. My head hurts with thinking.'

His mood had changed since he opened the door. He seemed anxious to talk. Quinn had seen it before. To a man in trouble any company was better than none.

. . . Probably not a bad fellow at heart. Trouble is she

preferred Harold Graham. We may never know how long the affaire had been going on. When the time came to choose finally between them, Harold's fifty-four thousand pounds tipped the scales in his favour ...

Quinn asked, 'Why don't you take some aspirins?'

'No, I'll be all right.' Marshall rubbed one hand in the other and looked up. 'I'd be out and about if I had wheels. Damn car won't be ready until tomorrow at the earliest.'

'Just as well, maybe. Give you a chance to get over your flu.'

'What flu? I just had a cold with a touch of backache. It was—' he made a sour face—'it was my wife who talked me into staying in bed yesterday. Said it would do me good ... and I could have my car serviced while I didn't need it. Now I know why she wanted me out of the way.'

'What difference would it have made?'

'I'm in town all this week. If she'd been working late as she said—and my car hadn't been in dock—I'd have called at the factory for her last night. And that would never have done ... would it?'

'No, it wouldn't,' Quinn said.

He wondered what good it would do to go on asking questions. She had lied to her husband to get him out of the way. He had become nothing more than an encumbrance. For weeks, or months, her life had been all lies.

Marshall said, 'I mentioned to the police what I've just told you and Superintendent Hennant saw it the same way as I do. She fooled me into believing she was concerned about my health.'

'That seems obvious,' Quinn said. 'But it doesn't get us any further. Was there nothing in her behaviour during the past few weeks to make you curious?'

'Not a thing. She was just as usual. This has come straight out of the blue. I never suspected anything ... not a thing. We were happy together. Seldom had a wrong word. I'd have staked my life there was no other man.'

... If she could fool him like she did he must be a prize idiot. This stunt couldn't have been planned overnight. It must've been brewing for a long time. Of course, he was

Q.W.

out of town a lot. She had plenty of opportunities to meet Graham. They might even have had some cosy sessions right here while hubby was away . . .

Quinn said, 'The police want every scrap of publicity they can get. My column in the *Morning Post* is pretty widely read only because I build it round the human element.'

Marshall stood up. He said, 'I'm sorry. I don't follow you. My head's a bit thick today. What is it you want to do?'

'I want to write about the personalities involved in this case—not just the theft of a large sum of money.'

'Oh, I see.' The look of doubt was in his eyes again. 'Well, I've no desire to be one of the personalities in a scandal and have my private life plastered all over the country.'

'You've got no private life,' Quinn said. 'You're part of the scandal—a major part. Your wife saw to that when she ran off with Harold Graham.'

'I know that without you telling me. If I could get my hands on him—'

'You won't . . . and neither will the police unless someone gives them the tip-off. This is the type of case where they have to rely on information received.'

'Well, I've given them all the information I possess,' Marshall said. 'They'll have to look somewhere else.'

'That's the big problem. They can't knock at the door of every house in every street from Land's End to John o' Groats. It's the ordinary member of the public who'll lead them to your wife and Harold Graham . . . with luck.'

Marshall's hands moved restlessly. He said, 'All right, you've made your point. I still don't know any more than you do.'

Quinn said, 'That's a strange remark for a husband to make. How long have you been married?'

'Eight years. What's that got to do with it?'

'Everything. You can't live with a woman all that time without learning a lot about her.'

'Maybe. But it won't help you to find where they've gone.'

'Leave me to decide that. Don't they deserve to be locked up instead of living it up?'

Marshall drew in a long deep breath. Then the tension slowly drained out of him.

In an apathetic voice, he said, 'Graham's going to get more than perhaps he deserves . . . but he doesn't know it yet. I can't make myself hate him. He's just a fool. Yvonne's the one behind this whole thing. She's merely used him as the means to an end. That's all.'

'Is she like that?'

'Oh, yes. To the outside world she's very sweet, very charming but inside she's as hard as iron. I know.'

'You should,' Quinn said.

Marshall fidgeted again. It seemed difficult for him to remain still.

He said, 'I've never talked about her like this before . . . never. But I don't owe her any loyalty, do I?'

'Not any more,' Quinn said.

'She's always had her own way. I suppose it was partly my fault but I didn't really mind. When I said we were happy together I meant it. Life might not have been quite the same as it was before—' he faltered and a hurt look came into his eyes—'before the accident, but I made allowances because she'd taken it badly . . .'

Without any emotion he went on as though forced by a compulsive need. Quinn felt it had been a long time since Keith Marshall unburdened himself to anyone. Now he had a captive audience.

'. . . She wasn't demonstrative and we weren't as close as we used to be while we had Peter. When he died we kind of drifted apart. I thought another child would make up for our loss but she wouldn't even consider it. In fact, she was so afraid it might happen she wouldn't let me come near her . . . if you know what I mean.'

Quinn said, 'Yes, I know.'

He was trying to understand how two people could go on living the kind of life the Marshalls must have had—married and yet living apart. It hardly mattered whose fault it had been.

... But Yvonne was a normal woman with a normal appetite. To satisfy it she took a lover. Maybe Graham represented more than sex to her. Maybe he had qualities she'd never found in her husband. Maybe Marshall reminded her too much of the dead child ... or she made that the excuse for not sharing his bed ...

Marshall said, 'She wasn't that way inclined ... so I'll swear she didn't go off with Graham because she wanted a man. You're wrong—everybody's wrong—to think she's his mistress. She wouldn't want him for that.'

'You know best,' Quinn said.

Nothing registered in Marshall's heavy face. In the same tone, he went on, 'When she's got her hands on that money, Graham won't see her again. He won't get a penny of it. I could almost feel sorry for him. He had a good job and a wife and a respected position ... and he's thrown it all away for damn all.'

'Keep your sympathy for yourself,' Quinn said. 'You need it more than he does. He took your wife—whatever their relationship may be—and he stole his firm's money. If what you say about her is true it serves him right.'

Marshall turned and stared through the window at the grey sky. For a long time he was silent.

When he looked at Quinn again, he said, 'Self-pity won't get me anywhere. Some people might say I was better off without her. For the past year or two it hasn't been much of a life for me, anyway.'

He gave a little shiver. Then he added, 'I think I'll have another drink.'

Quinn asked, 'How many have you had?'

'A couple ... maybe three. Never touch the stuff in the morning ... but today's different. I'd get blind paralytic if I thought it would help.'

'It won't. This thing will look even worse when you see it through a hangover. You've got to face realities.'

Marshall nodded. He said, 'Easy for you to talk. Are you married?'

'No.'

'Big deal. What gives you the right to preach at me? I let

you into my home and answer your questions and in return you look down your nose at me. Well, you can go to hell. You can—'

He stopped with his mouth hanging open. Then he slumped into a chair and put both hands over his mouth.

Through his fingers, he mumbled, 'I'm sorry. I didn't mean to say that. Don't go. Have a drink with me and stay a little while.'

The jaded voice in Quinn's head began nagging him again. '... *That's right, you do. Why not? It's free. You can get pickled at somebody else's expense. He'll weep in his glass and you can weep in yours. Before the day's over, Marshall will have lost his wife and you'll have lost your job* ...'

Quinn said, 'No, thanks, not for me. But I'll get you one. Where do you keep it?'

'In the sideboard—right-hand cupboard. You'll find glasses there, too.'

It was a well-stocked cupboard. At the front stood a bottle of whisky three-quarters full with a glass beside it that Quinn saw had been used.

He poured out a stiff drink and handed it to Marshall. This was as good a way as any to keep the man talking. And it would serve a double purpose. When he had talked it out of his system he would feel much better.

With the glass held in both hands, Marshall sat looking into the distance, his eyes flat and empty. Then he tilted back his head and poured half the whisky down his throat.

Quinn asked, 'Had any breakfast this morning?'

'No, I couldn't eat.' He finished the rest of the whisky, balanced his glass on the arm of the chair and shook his head. 'I'm not the least bit hungry.'

'When did you last eat?'

'Yesterday evening. Made myself a bite. Not much ... because I thought Yvonne would be home soon and—' He left the next word in mid-air.

'Alcohol on an empty stomach can make you do some damn silly things,' Quinn said. 'Take it easy with that stuff.'

'Why? It can't make me do anything more stupid than I did eight years ago when I got married.'

He got up and carried his glass over to the sideboard and helped himself to another double whisky. When he had taken a sip he looked at Quinn and asked, 'Sure you won't have one?'

'Quite sure, thanks.'

'Go on, have a drop of scotch. What harm can it do you?'

'I'm a working lad,' Quinn said.

'So am I. But not today. Ordinarily I should've been at the office but—' He cupped his hands around the glass and stared down at the floor.

'Does your firm know what's happened?'

'Yes, I phoned the sales manager at nine o'clock.'

'What did he say?'

Marshall looked up and took a quick drink. He said, 'That's a foolish question. What could he say? When he'd made all the right noises he advised me to take a couple of days off and get things straightened out. You would've thought I'd told him we'd had a burst pipe.'

'It's always difficult for someone who knows you,' Quinn said. 'Talking to a stranger is less embarrassing.'

'Especially a sympathetic stranger.' Marshall smiled with one side of his mouth. 'That's why I'm glad you came.'

'Because you think I'm sorry for you?'

'No, because I'm quite sure you're not. You don't care a damn about me. Why should you? This is just part of a day's work. You called here to get an interview with Yvonne Marshall's husband and you got one—a complete life story. So, good for you.'

Quinn said, 'You're wrong. There isn't a line in the whole interview that I could publish. All I've done is provide you with company while you're feeling low. Not very profitable from my news editor's point of view.'

The look on Marshall's face changed. He said, 'I didn't mean to open a big mouth. If I could help you I would. Not that I care a damn what happens to my wife and that man Graham. It makes no odds to me whether the police catch them or they get away with the money they stole. I never want to see her again, anyway.'

He emptied his glass and put it down on the floor. Then he added, 'Don't suppose I'm likely to. By now they're probably out of the country.'

'There is that chance,' Quinn said. 'On the other hand they might still be here ... possibly even in London.'

'Not unless they're out of their minds. With all that money they could get—'

'This is a big city. Two people can lose themselves among eight million. All they have to do is change their appearances slightly and live like any normal couple.'

Marshall sat feeling his cheek while he thought. He said, 'The police asked me if she'd ever bought a wig. Lots of women wear them. Superintendent Hennant thinks it's quite possible she had one made months ago all ready for the time she'd need it to disappear.'

'But she would make sure you never saw it,' Quinn said.

'That's what I told the superintendent. She'd have been stupid to leave the thing lying around. And whatever else she might be—' his face darkened—'she isn't stupid. I'm the fool. I'd never have believed she could do this to me.'

'You're being an even bigger fool now,' Quinn said.

With his hand stroking his cheek Marshall looked at him and asked, 'In what way?'

'You know what way. If she weren't wanted by the police she could walk in right now and you'd take her back.'

The tired look deepened in Marshall's face. He said, 'It's not true. I've finished with her.'

'No, you haven't. You'd be prepared to forgive and forget so long as you could be sure of one thing—that she hadn't given Graham what she'd withheld from you.'

Marshall shook his head. After two attempts, he said, 'I keep remembering that we've been married for the past eight years, that we went through hell together when Peter was killed. It seems wrong that it should all end—like this.'

Quinn said, 'It is wrong. But that doesn't alter the situation. You can't go on kidding yourself ...'

There his argument lost impetus. He realized he was

interfering in another man's intimate affairs. It was not his business to tell Marshall how he should feel.

In any case the whole thing was an academic exercise. Yvonne had no intention of coming back. What her husband would, or would not, do was quite immaterial.

In a strained voice, Marshall said, 'Perhaps you're right. I don't care what she's done. I can overlook anything providing she hasn't been Graham's mistress.'

Quinn told himself it was time he got out of this house. He had no wish to hear any more bedroom revelations.

. . . This fellow doesn't seem to have any self-respect. Not that you should've got him going. He only needed you to say he'd take her back if she hadn't slept with Graham. Bet he'd have a fit if he knew you suspected that his wife left him because he'd become impotent . . .

Marshall asked, 'Can you imagine what it's like to live in the same house with a woman who behaves as if you were her brother?'

'I can imagine,' Quinn said.

He wished he could have heard Yvonne's side of the story. There was always another side. Pity he would never know what she had gone through during those eight years of marriage.

It might not have been her idea to rob the company. Money could well have been less important to her than getting away from husband and home.

But she would need money to escape. And there was a fortune to be had for the taking . . . if she could persuade Harold Graham to co-operate.

Maybe she had never been in love with him. Maybe Marshall was right. She had used Graham as the means to an end.

It scarcely mattered now. They had planned and executed the theft with professional skill. If their escape arrangements were anywhere near as perfect, they had every chance of getting clean away.

As though he could read Quinn's thoughts, Marshall said, 'I'm just being damn silly. What's the use of saying what I'd do if she came back? It won't ever happen. They've gone

... and the police haven't a hope of catching them. I'll never see her again.'

'I'm inclined to agree with you,' Quinn said. 'But one thing I know: Scotland Yard will go on trying. They don't give up all that easily. Add a spot of luck to a lot of persistence and anything can happen.'

Marshall said, 'I'll believe it when I see it. Meantime I've enough worries of my own. Wherever I go people will be talking about me behind my back. I don't know how I'm going to live it down.'

'You will. Who knows? In your job it might even be good for business.'

'I can do without that sort of thing.'

'Probably... but no one will hold it against you,' Quinn said. 'Now I'll have to be on my way.'

'Sure you won't have a drink?'

'Daren't risk it. I'm calling on a lady—Harold Graham's wife.'

Marshall waited until Quinn had reached the door before he said, 'I'd completely forgotten about her. Wonder how she feels?'

'Badly shaken up, I imagine. She must've had as big a shock as you did.'

'Yes, I suppose so.' He shook his head. 'Damn shame. Has she got any kids?'

'No. If she had it would be pretty rough on them.'

'Never thought of that,' Marshall said. 'What does a woman do when her husband goes off with somebody else?'

Quinn said, 'She can sue for maintenance. The court will grant her a reasonable slice of her husband's income but no one guarantees she'll be able to collect. In this case it would obviously be a waste of time.'

In a distant voice, Marshall repeated, 'Damn shame...'

Then he went over to the sideboard and brought out the bottle of whisky and half-filled his glass. When he had taken a sip he looked at Quinn and said, 'Here have I been thinking I was badly done to. But she's in a lot worse trouble... and through no fault of her own.'

'You can say that again,' Quinn said.

As he walked down to the gate he was asking himself if Marshall realized the significance of that last remark. It was an admission in itself.

'... *through no fault of her own.*'

Only one construction could be put on his words. Mrs Graham had given her husband no reason to leave her. But that was not the situation between Marshall and his wife. Yvonne must have had more than enough reason. And he knew it only too well.

... Seems to like children. Could be that the loss of their little boy had a bigger effect on Marshall than it had on his wife. Maybe I got it back to front: he was the one who blamed her. If she were supposed to collect the boy from school and she hadn't picked him up that day ...

The tangled lives of this ill-suited pair could explain why Yvonne had got out when the chance presented itself. But in the long run motive was unimportant. It gave no clue to where she had gone when she drove away from the Jauncey Engineering Company's factory.

In the depths of Quinn's mind he could hear Marshall saying '... *When she's got her hands on that money, Graham won't see her again ...*'

Marshall knew what his wife was capable of doing. Perhaps he would have talked less freely if he had not had too much to drink.

Behind the echo of his voice there was an elusive thought. When Quinn at last pinned it down he had a new concept of what might have happened.

... Two cars were parked outside the Administration block. Yvonne Marshall loaded the stolen money into one of them—the one she was going to drive. The other was Graham's getaway car ...

But they had not needed two cars to make their escape with the money. So the second one served another purpose ... if its ownership could not be traced.

The registration number of Graham's car was known. It had to be abandoned before the theft was discovered.

... Suppose Yvonne Marshall arranged to pick up Graham when he had planted the decoy car? The pair of them

could then head wherever they fancied, secure in the knowledge that there was nothing to link them with the second car. But that assumes they'd got hold of a vehicle which no one knew they were using . . . and I don't see how they managed it . . .

If his theory was worth anything he had no right to keep it to himself. Other people might have had the same idea but it cost him nothing to find out.

He stopped at a phone box on Dollis Hill Lane and rang Piper's office. When he got no reply he realized it was lunchtime . . . and he had gone without breakfast . . . and he knew a pub in Willesden where the beer was good and the sandwiches edible.

But first he had another call to make. It was important to get his priorities right. It was even more important to keep in with the Law.

CHAPTER V

DETECTIVE-SUPERINTENDENT HENNANT SAID, 'I don't think we've met before, Mr Quinn, but I often read your feature in the *Morning Post*. Quinn's Column on Crime is more or less the first thing I turn to when I open the paper.'

He had sharp blue eyes and the complexion of a man who lived an outdoor life. He looked like a farmer or a ship's officer or a fisherman. Quinn had the thought that he might even have been a gamekeeper—or a poacher.

'Nice to know,' Quinn said. 'If you put it in writing I might get a rise.'

Hennant smiled the kind of polite smile that meant nothing. He said, 'I really do enjoy your column. Interesting stuff . . . most interesting. However, you're a busy man and I mustn't waste your time. What is this idea you want to discuss with me?'

Quinn said, 'I've been talking to Yvonne Marshall's husband. Got to the house not long after you left.'

'Oh, yes? And what did he have to say?'

'Well, he told me the sad story of his life. Their marriage —according to him—wasn't exactly a state of wedded bliss.'

'I got that impression, too,' Hennant said. 'Of course, I'd anticipated something of the kind. A woman who's happily married doesn't run off with another man.'

'I'm not sure she did,' Quinn said.

Superintendent Hennant showed no surprise. In the same controlled voice, he asked, 'Are you saying she didn't take part in the theft of the Jauncey Engineering Company's payroll?'

'Oh, no, I'm not saying that. She took part all right. But I've got a hunch she didn't run off with Harold Graham.'

Hennant murmured, 'I see . . .' Then he sat plucking at his thick lower lip with no expression on his face.

From time to time he made little tuneless sounds as though trying to recall a thread of melody. Quinn wondered if anyone had ever told him it was an irritating habit.

At last the superintendent let go of his lip and asked, 'Am I right in assuming that you think they split up when they left the factory?'

Quinn said, 'Yes . . . but only in the sense that they parted company. I don't believe they split the money. Judging by what her husband says about her she was only in it for the cash.'

'Meaning it's possible she tricked Graham?'

'More than possible—if Marshall's assessment of her can be relied upon.'

'Is he reliable or just mud-slinging because of the way he's been treated?'

'He'd had quite a lot to drink and, in that state, I'd be inclined to accept that what he said about her was basically true.'

Hennant looked doubtful. He said, 'I wouldn't be too sure. I got the impression he hated her for what she'd done to him.'

Quinn said, 'So did I at first. But when he'd had another couple of stiff whiskies I came to the conclusion it was one of those love-hate things. They haven't slept together for the past couple of years . . . and he insists she isn't Graham's mistress. Apparently she's not the sexy type.'

With another polite smile, Hennant said, 'You seem to have gained his confidence, Mr Quinn. He never discussed his sex life with me.'

'Maybe you weren't particularly interested.'

'Well, it hardly seemed relevant. The facts were plain enough. She'd left her husband and gone off with another man after robbing the firm where she and her lover worked.'

'If he was her lover,' Quinn said.

Superintendent Hennant raised his eyebrows. In an amiable voice, he asked, 'Is it important? Does it really matter what the relationship is between them?'

'I think it may affect your chances of catching them.'

'How?'

'Because the police and the public are on the lookout for two people living together. If my hunch—based on what Marshall told me—is correct then she's in some nice cosy hideout with fifty-four thousand pounds under the mattress while he's left high and dry with not a sausage.'

'That's pure conjecture,' Hennant said. 'The factory patrolman—who's our only witness—says two cars were parked outside Admin. Evidently Graham and Mrs Marshall needed both vehicles for their plan to succeed. We don't know what that plan was—but we can be pretty sure it was one they'd mutually agreed on.'

Quinn said, 'My guess is that she was to drive straight to their hiding-place while he dumped his own car in a spot as far away from that place as possible.'

'Where we'd find it and assume they'd gone in that direction?'

'Of course.'

'But we haven't found it. There's no trace of either car. How do you explain that?'

'I don't,' Quinn said. 'I can only imagine something went wrong with their plan.'

'Such as what?'

'Maybe Graham woke up to the fact that she meant to

double-cross him.'

'Again presupposing that she did,' Hennant said.

He leaned forward and rested his big muscular hands on the desk. Then he went on, 'Let's ask ourselves something that is relevant, Mr Quinn. Why should they let us know that two cars were involved? They didn't need to. They could've left the factory together in Graham's car, driven to some place where a second car was parked and transferred themselves and the money to the other vehicle. Right?'

'Quite right,' Quinn said.

'And the answer?'

'There's only one that I can suggest. They didn't care how much you knew once they'd got away.'

'Which means they had no further use for either car. And that might indicate they hadn't far to go.'

'Or they were switching to an alternative form of transport,' Quinn said.

Superintendent Hennant bobbed his head in agreement. He said, 'Sea or air . . . I hope not. It leaves the whole wide world open to them. I prefer your original theory.'

'So do I. But I wish somebody would tell me how and where they disposed of the two cars. Graham's bound to have got rid of the one that's registered in his name. He had plenty of time before the theft was discovered and he could've left it anywhere.'

'All he had to do was pull up in some quiet street, get out and walk away,' Hennant said.

Quinn sat looking at the empty ashtray on the superintendent's desk. It had been wiped clean and polished until it shone.

. . . No one who smokes has an ashtray like that. Expect it's just kept for the use of visitors. Not much good asking for a cigarette . . .

He said, 'That goes for Mrs Marshall, too. Wherever she got hold of her car it's a constant liability. She had to dump it somewhere as soon as possible after she'd unloaded Jauncey's payroll money.'

'We don't know who was driving which,' Hennant said.

'Not that it matters at this stage. My concern is what they did with them.'

'Possibly stuck them in a lock-up somewhere.'

'But why?'

Quinn said, 'If I knew that I'd be in the running for a nice fat reward. And while we're on the subject, what kind of insurance cover has the firm got?'

'A money policy.'

'Any special conditions?'

'No, it doesn't exclude collusion either by forceful methods or otherwise. They paid a bit more for it but they were covered up to sixty thousand pounds, whoever stole the money and however it was done.'

With curiosity brightening his sharp blue eyes, Hennant asked, 'Why do you want to know?'

'Just wondered,' Quinn said. 'I suppose there'll be a ten per cent reward offered as usual?'

'Yes, it'll be advertised in tomorrow morning's *Telegraph* and *Times* and one or two other papers.'

The superintendent leaned back and stretched. Then he added, 'Not that it'll do much good in this case. No one to grass.'

'I had that thought myself,' Quinn said. 'Ordinary thieving is bad enough but you've got a real job on here . . . especially if Mrs Yvonne Marshall has pulled a fast one on Graham and taken a solo trip to parts unknown.'

Hennant said, 'You depress me, Mr Quinn. I've enough on my plate without worrying about that sort of possibility.'

'It may be more than a possibility,' Quinn said.

He told himself he had let the idea become almost an obsession. He would achieve more if he could explain how two cars had disappeared.

 . . . Yet it would've been so easy for Yvonne to ditch her accomplice. If she were driving the car in which she'd loaded the money she just had to keep going. When Graham arrived at the place where they'd arranged to meet she wouldn't be there. And he could do nothing about it . . .

Perhaps he would be able to lie low for a time in the hideout they had set up before the theft was carried out.

But whatever money he had would be exhausted before long.

To find Yvonne meant coming out into the open. That was asking to be picked up. So all he could do was hide like a hunted animal, afraid day and night that he would do something to betray himself.

... When his money runs out he'll have to scrounge every bite to eat. End up living rough like a drop-out. In that sort of state he doesn't stand a cat-in-hell chance of finding her. Meanwhile the police will go on seeking a woman in the company of a man—not a woman living on her own in a place where she has a completely new identity ...

Superintendent Hennant said, 'Well, I'll bear it in mind, Mr Quinn. If you have any more ideas I'll always be glad to hear them.'

'It's not ideas you need,' Quinn said. 'It's positive information. Mind if I give you a ring now and again to see if you've found those two cars?'

'Not at all. In case I'm not available have a word with Sergeant Freeson.'

Quinn could guess what that meant. Any time he phoned he would be shunted to an underling.

He said, 'Thanks. I'll remember that ...'

Maryland Avenue, Crouch End, was a leaf-strewn road lined on both sides with overhanging trees. There was a grass verge between each set of gates. The houses were detached, secluded and substantial.

Few of them had numbers. A greengrocer's roundsman told Quinn the Grahams lived at Elm Haven.

The name plaque hung by a chain in the arched entrance. On either side of the doorway stood empty flower-tubs.

There was a car parked in front of the double garage—a two-door Triumph convertible. By its registration index it was three years old.

Before Quinn reached the entrance, the door opened. A blonde young woman asked, 'Yes? Who is it you want?'

He said, 'My name's Quinn. Are you Mrs Graham?'

'No, I'm Miss Field, her sister. If you tell me your business I may be able to help you.'

'I doubt it,' Quinn said. 'I've called in connection with her missing husband.'

'Oh . . .' Miss Field drew back a little. 'Do you mean he's been found?'

She had fluffy hair, warm brown eyes and pretty teeth. Quinn thought she was nice to look at.

. . . Nearer thirty than twenty-five . . . smart-looking piece . . . speaks well and has plenty of self-confidence. Bet she'd know how to handle any man who tried to get fresh with her . . .

He said, 'Not yet. So far there's no sign of either Graham or Mrs Marshall. I was hoping I might learn something from his wife about the background to this affair.'

'The police have already been here. She's told them she doesn't know a thing and it's all been a terrible shock to her. I don't see why she should be upset again by more questioning.'

'I'm not from the police,' Quinn said. 'But I've just left Superintendent Hennant of Scotland Yard and he gave me the impression there might be something he'd omitted to ask your sister. So if she could spare me a couple of minutes I'd be very grateful.'

With a colder look in her eyes, Miss Field said, 'I think you'd better explain what you mean. Did the superintendent send you?'

'No, but—'

'A straightforward no is sufficient. Was he aware that you intended to question Mrs Graham?'

'It doesn't matter whether he was or he wasn't,' Quinn said. 'There's no law to stop me.'

'Perhaps not. But I can stop you. Unless I'm mistaken you're a newspaper reporter.'

'What gives you that idea?'

'You look like one.'

Quinn said, 'That's a slur on the whole profession . . . but we'll let it pass. What have you got against reporters?'

In a brisk voice, Miss Field said, 'I've neither the time

nor the inclination to enter into a debate with you. My sister has had quite enough for one day without being pestered by anyone from a newspaper. So please go away. If you don't—'

'No need to threaten me,' Quinn said. 'In the course of my career I've been requested to leave by some of the best people. Most of them were polite because they could respect a man who was merely doing an honest job. You're different. Evidently you suspect that my intentions are dishonest.'

Miss Field looked momentarily uncomfortable. She said, 'I didn't say that. I only asked you to go away. My sister has nothing to say to you.'

'How do you know? Don't you think she should be given the opportunity to say so herself?'

'It would merely vex her for no reason. Can't you understand how distressing all this has been?'

Quinn said, 'Yes, I can understand. I can also see you don't feel very happy about this trick your brother-in-law has played on everybody.'

Her mouth tightened. She said, 'I'd rather not talk about him.'

'Why not? It can't do your sister any harm . . . and you don't owe him anything. The quicker he's caught and locked up, the quicker this thing will die a natural death. And that's where you can help.'

She studied Quinn with the same cold look in her eyes. Then she asked, 'How? What can I do . . . or you either, for that matter?'

'Maybe a lot, maybe nothing at all. But I can tell you that the police are scratching around for any scrap of information they can pick up.'

'They won't get it from me . . . because I haven't the faintest idea where he's gone.'

'Nevertheless, you know him pretty well. There might just be some tiny detail that could give a lead to—'

'Then you'll have to look for it somewhere else,' Miss Field said. 'I neither know nor care what happens to Harold

Graham. Nothing's too bad for a man who can behave as he has done.'

Quinn said, 'May I ask you one small question?'

The cold look thawed into doubt. She said, 'That depends on what you want to know.'

'Oh, nothing very terrible. I just wondered if you'd ever suspected that Graham was having an affaire.'

She took her hand off the edge of the door and held it to her mouth while she stood thinking. At last, she said, 'What difference does it make? The police aren't hunting for him because he's been an unfaithful husband. He's a thief.'

'Are you sure he's been unfaithful?'

Her look of doubt vanished. She said, 'Oh, come! You're not suggesting they're just good friends, are you?'

'I'm not in a position to suggest anything,' Quinn said. 'But after what a man called Marshall told me I wouldn't be in a hurry to say that Mrs Marshall and your brother-in-law were lovers.'

'What—' Miss Field was no longer sure of herself—'what did he tell you?'

'Enough to make me feel there was nothing between his wife and Graham other than a business partnership,' Quinn said.

She wrapped both arms round herself and shivered in the draught through the half-open door. Then she said, 'If I thought that was true . . .'

Quinn waited with the patience of long experience. They always started off by saying they had nothing to say. But when the bait was tempting enough they seldom could resist it. In this case, family loyalty, a sense of duty, would provide the incentive to talk.

It may have been the growing cold of late afternoon that made up her mind. She said, 'We can't stand here like this . . . and I'd like to hear what it's all about. But Mrs Graham's resting so you'll have to keep your voice down.'

'Of course,' Quinn said.

She let him in only as far as the hall. It was a place of warmth and half-light and solid old furniture.

After she had closed the door quietly she came round to face him. She said, 'There's one thing we must get clear before we go any further. Whatever the relationship may have been between this woman Marshall and my brother-in-law doesn't affect the main issue: he's stolen money from his employers and he's left his wife.'

'I wouldn't argue about the theft,' Quinn said. 'But the other bit might not be as cut-and-dried as it appears.'

'How can you say that? He's gone, hasn't he?'

'Oh, yes. But he could be intending to send for his wife when all the excitement has died down.'

With a trace of irritation, Miss Field said, 'You can't be so naïve as to believe that. First of all he kept my sister in complete ignorance of what he was planning to do: secondly he understands her well enough to know she would never be a party to what he's done. She wouldn't touch stolen money.'

'What do you think she'd do if he communicated with her?'

'That's a hypothetical question. He never will.'

'But suppose he did? Suppose he told her where he was hiding out? Would she inform the police?'

Miss Field moved restlessly. She said, 'I can't answer that. I'm not my sister. I only know what I'd do if I were in her position.'

'But that's the whole point—you're not. You wouldn't feel sorry for him if you found out he was in serious trouble.'

'There's no if about it. He is in serious trouble. When the police catch him—'

'I didn't mean that kind of trouble,' Quinn said. 'From what Marshall told me about his wife I've got a hunch she's gone off with the money and Harold Graham won't see a penny of it.'

After a long silence, Miss Field said, 'He wouldn't be such a fool as to let himself be tricked like that.'

'He might—if he were infatuated with someone as attractive as Yvonne Marshall.'

'But you told me—'

'—that their relationship was only a business one. And

her husband thinks it was because that was how she wanted it to be. But no one knows what Graham's feelings were towards her.'

'We can guess,' Miss Field said.

She gave Quinn a long steady look. In a voice tinged with bitterness, she asked, 'Why does a man throw away everything because a woman smiles at him? Why does he destroy himself, humiliate his wife, degrade his family? What gets into him for no reason at all?'

'There's always a reason,' Quinn said. 'Not all marriages are made in heaven.'

'If you're saying that my sister and her husband were unsuited to each other you're wrong. They were very much in love. From the day they met he thought she was wonderful . . . and she was devoted to him.'

'How long have they been married?'

'Nearly thirteen years. She was just turned twenty and he was thirty-two. In all that time I've never known them to have a cross word.'

'Do you live here?'

'No, I have a flat in town. But if you're thinking—'

'I'm thinking only that no one knows what goes on between a husband and wife when they're alone,' Quinn said. 'And something I read a while ago might interest you. Statistics show that divorce or separation is more likely around the fourteenth year of marriage than at any other period.'

Miss Field shrugged and said nothing. When she just went on looking at him, Quinn added, 'Seems to be a common pattern of behaviour after that length of time. The article didn't say whether it was the husband or the wife who had a change of mind.'

'It wasn't the wife in this case,' Miss Field said.

'How can you be sure?'

'Because my sister refuses to believe what the police told her. She insists there's been some mistake. Harold wouldn't rob anybody. Harold wouldn't leave her for some other woman. If he walked in right now he could make any excuse he liked and—'

'—and she'd still take him back,' Quinn said.

. . . That makes two of them. Marshall trusts his wife, Mrs Graham has faith in her husband. If the runaways are never found, their respective spouses will keep a lamp in the window to the end of their days. Must be something about marriage that causes softening of the brain . . .

Miss Field nodded. She said, 'Of course, everybody else knows there isn't the slightest chance of his coming back . . . at least, not of his own accord. But supposing he did? Supposing he finds out that this woman Marshall has tricked him? If he decides that he's made a terrible blunder and gives himself up, what will happen to him?'

'All depends,' Quinn said.

'On what?'

'On fifty-four thousand pounds. If he helped the police to recover Jauncey Engineering Company's payroll he might get a suspended sentence. Of course, if the police laid their hands on him first . . .'

'He'd go to prison for a long time,' Miss Field said.

She walked to the foot of the stairs and listened for a moment as though she had heard a sound in one of the upstairs rooms. Then she tip-toed back.

In a quiet voice, she said, 'You seem to be an intelligent person. Do you really believe what this man Marshall told you?'

'I believe that he believes it,' Quinn said.

'But that doesn't mean it's true?'

'No . . . just possible.'

'If it is true, then Harold will have found out for himself by this time, won't he?'

'You can bet on that,' Quinn said. 'Where do we go from here?'

She looked at him with a remote light in her eyes. She said, 'If Mrs Marshall has tricked him out of the money, he won't know where she's gone, will he?'

'No. That's his big problem.'

'Then what would he achieve by giving himself up? There's no way he can help the police.'

'Not unless he's got some idea where she might be.'

'But, if he has, why doesn't he go there?'

'Because he may be scared of coming out into the open,' Quinn said.

'By the time he thinks it's safe to make a move, she can have transferred herself and the money to some other place—some place where he'll never find her.'

'That's what must be giving him ulcers right now,' Quinn said. 'This is all supposition but, if there is anything in it, time certainly isn't on his side.'

Miss Field glanced over her shoulder. When she turned to Quinn again, she said, 'Nobody can appreciate what this has done to my sister. For her sake, there's very little I wouldn't do to get Harold out of the mess he's got himself into.'

'But not for his sake,' Quinn said. 'Why don't you like him?'

'There's no question of like or dislike. He's my sister's husband. That doesn't mean we've got to be friends.'

'All the same, it's usual. What has he done to make you feel the way you do?'

In the failing light she stared beyond Quinn, her eyes troubled. At last, she said, 'I don't see why that should be any of your business.'

'It is—if you want my help.'

'How can you help me or my sister? You're only in this because you want a story for—what's the name of the paper you work for?'

'The *Morning Post*. And you're quite right. I wouldn't have become involved if it weren't my job. That doesn't mean I can't have a personal interest as well. Believe it or not, newspaper men are almost human.'

She looked at him steadily as though trying to read his thoughts. She said, 'If you must know, I've been worried for months about my brother-in-law.'

'Why?'

'He's been coming home late several nights a week. Told my sister he had business meetings to attend. Previously it was only on an odd occasion but in recent times it had become a regular occurrence.'

'Did she ask him why he was suddenly needed so often?'

'Yes. The reason he gave her was that the works manager was making frequent trips abroad on export negotiations and someone had to stand in for him at these works conferences.'

'Was this happening every week?'

'No, for a couple of weeks at a time and then there'd be a week when he'd be home at his usual hour.'

'That would be the week Marshall wasn't away on his travels,' Quinn said. 'He's a commercial representative and out of town a lot but occasionally he spends a few days at the London office.'

'And lives at home,' Miss Field said. Her eyes seemed to have gathered shadows from the growing darkness of the hall.

'Yes. So his wife couldn't entertain her man friend.'

'In other words, I was right. Harold was lying to my sister. This Marshall woman must've been his mistress.'

'Well, if he visited her on the nights he was supposed to be working late, I'd make a guess they weren't playing snakes-and-ladders.'

'But—' Miss Field broke off and began again. 'That makes nonsense of what her husband told you.'

'Husbands can be as blind as wives,' Quinn said.

She stood looking at him in silence. He asked, 'How long will you be staying here?'

'Only overnight. My boss has given me today off but I'll have to be at the office tomorrow morning without fail.'

'Can I get in touch with you there . . . if something new turns up?'

'Yes, I'll let you have my phone number. You can ring me any time during the day except between one and two . . .'

He had no intention of phoning her but he scribbled the number in his dog-eared notebook. She had already told him what he wanted to know: Mrs Graham would be alone in the house next day.

As he let himself out, Miss Field asked, 'Have you thought that Mrs Marshall might've let Harold become her lover for this very purpose? If she did, what her husband says about her wouldn't be so far wrong.'

Quinn said, 'Maybe you've got something there. Wouldn't be the first time a woman has fooled a man into getting her what she wants and then tossed him to the wolves.'

He was wondering why this nice-looking blonde kept playing variations on the same theme: Harold Graham was an adulterous husband. Whether the other woman had tricked him or not, Harold had been unfaithful to his wife.

. . . Maybe that's what she wants her sister to believe. Maybe she isn't altogether displeased that he's gone off. Could be she's always disliked Graham . . .

He went out on to the porch. When he turned to say goodbye, Miss Field asked, 'What do you think a man would do if he were treated—like that?'

To Quinn it seemed a loaded question. He said, 'Depends on the sort of man he is. In his shoes I'd want to make her pay . . . and not just for doing me out of my share of the money. It's the other deceit that would hurt me more.'

'Yes, I can understand that.' She came a step nearer. 'And I know Harold. Normally he's a good-natured man. But he has a temper when he's roused.'

'They're the worst kind,' Quinn said. 'One of these days Yvonne Marshall may discover that to her cost.'

CHAPTER VI

It was half-past five when he got back to the office. He phoned Piper but there was no reply and he told himself it would keep till morning. He already knew what sort of insurance cover Jauncey Engineering Company had. In any case he had done enough for one day.

The Three Feathers would be open. After a pint or two he could have a meal in the staff canteen and then decide how he would spend the evening. It might be an idea to get to bed early for a change . . .

When he thought about it he realized he had no taste for beer. He had no appetite, either. What he did have was a headache and pains in the back of his neck like neuralgia.

Before six o'clock his hands and feet felt too big, his knees ached and he found it difficult to swallow. Someone passing his table asked him if he preferred interment or cremation.

'. . . You look like the ghost of Hamlet's father. Shouldn't be surprised if you've got flu. There's a lot of it about.'

'To coin a phrase,' Quinn said.

He took a dose of aspirin and washed it down with half a cup of hot tea. His stomach refused the other half. His stomach also hinted that it might reject the aspirins as well.

By then he knew the only place for him was bed. He told the man in Features to tell the news editor he might not be in next day.

'. . . If he doesn't see me he'll know why. Just say I feel lousy.'

The man in Features said, 'You look it, too. Nothing trivial, I hope?'

The journey home seemed endless. His head was hot, his hands and feet felt like ice. Now the aching had spread to every joint in his body.

As he sat shivering in the train he knew he should have taken a taxi. The underground was filled with noise that hurt—noise and light, the vertigo that swept over him each time the train ground to a halt, each time it accelerated out of the station. And ahead lay a walk through chill and windswept streets.

He had felt all right at five o'clock: no aches or pains, no sensation of nausea. Only an hour later he was a sick man. Something must have bitten him. He had it bad.

'. . . *Shouldn't be surprised if you've got flu. There's a lot of it about.*'

Everybody was fond of dishing out free medical opinions. Any fool could tell he had flu. Diagnosis was no help.

He counted the number of times the doors hissed open . . .

and hissed shut again. It was better than trying to catch the name of the station as the signs flitted past. They only made his head swim and brought on a renewed feeling of sickness.

... Damn funny how these things happen. Right as rain one minute and half-dead the next. In the midst of life ... Don't be so bloody morbid. Anybody would think you had bubonic plague ...

It was over at last. But the worst was still to come. As he set off to walk the remaining few hundred yards the cold wrapped itself around him and sucked the strength out of his bones.

He trudged on, hands deep in his pockets, his raincoat flapping in the wind. *Not long now ... not long now ...* The words kept in time with his footsteps.

Then he was climbing the steps and using his key on the front door. He had made it.

Mrs Buchanan fussed over him just as she always fussed. She put a hot-water bottle in his bed, brought him a scalding drink of rum and honey; insisted on sending for the doctor.

'... Ah'm no having you deeing in ma hoose. It's gey bad for business. Folks'll think Ah poison ma boarders ...'

Quinn was in no state to argue. When she had gone downstairs he lay sweating and shivering until the warmth of the bottle lulled him into an uneasy sleep.

More than once his headache wakened him. More than once he thought of a man called Marshall.

It must have been Marshall who had given him the flu in spite of what he said: '... *I just had a cold with a touch of backache ...*'

One man's cold was another man's influenza. Maybe the virus became more potent as it travelled from one victim to the next.

When he dozed off again he could hear some fool saying '... *There's a lot of it about.*'

Then the voice was a different voice. And someone had switched the light on. Through half-shut eyes he saw Mrs Buchanan bustling about.

'... The doctor's here, Mr Quinn. Ye'll soon be all right ... so dinna fret.'

Quinn said, 'Two-thirds of those present don't share your confidence.'

Then a flabby face looked down at him. Dr Young asked, 'Well, now, what have you been up to?'

'Silly questions get silly answers,' Quinn said.

'Oh, so that's the sort of mood we're in, is it? Stick out your tongue. If nothing else, it'll keep you quiet.'

He took Quinn's temperature, checked his pulse, sounded his chest. When the examination was over, he said, 'You'll live. Fasten your pyjama jacket.'

Quinn asked, 'What have I got?'

'Will it make you feel any better if we give it a label? As the immortal bard said: *A rose by any other name ...*'

'No, he didn't.'

'Really?' Dr Young plumped himself down on the edge of the bed and folded his arms over his fat chest. 'I always understood he did.'

'Well, you always understood wrong. The quotation is: *That which we call a rose, by any other name would smell as sweet.* It's from *Romeo and Juliet.*'

'You are a smart lad, aren't you?'

'No, not very. I only hope your medical knowledge is better than your Shakespeare.'

Young said, 'We'll soon find out, won't we? Perhaps I'll get the chance to recite: *Alas, poor Yorick. I knew him, Horatio; a fellow of infinite jest* ... No, maybe not. Couldn't say that about you.'

In the same tone, he went on, 'You've got a temperature and your throat's slightly inflamed ... but that won't last. Stay in bed, drink plenty and keep your bowels open.'

The pounding in Quinn's head was like the sullen beat of a drum. He asked, 'Is that all?'

'What do you want—a heart transplant?'

'Isn't there something I can take for my headache and the pains in my legs and back and damn near all over?'

'Yes. Three aspirins every four hours.'

'I could've done as much as that without letting Mrs Buchanan send for you.'

'Of course you could. Patients like you are mostly a waste of my valuable time. There was a good programme on TV this evening.'

Quinn said, 'And you lot call yourselves dedicated healers.'

Dr Young's flabby face creased in a smile that half-closed his eyes. He said, 'We don't, you know. That was before National Health. Now we're what one trade union leader called glorified plumbers—without the glory.'

'I don't think he's far wrong. When a patient can't even ask what he's suffering from . . .'

'OK. If it'll make you happy, go ahead and ask.'

'Nothing will make me happy. I just want to know if I've got flu.'

'Probably.'

Quinn said, 'You always back the horse both ways, don't you? Just for once, can't you say definitely what's wrong with me?'

'No.'

'Why not? You're a doctor, aren't you?'

'Oh, yes. But I'm not a psychiatrist.'

'Very hilarious,' Quinn said. 'Some day, if you're not careful, you'll commit yourself to a positive diagnosis.'

'You can have a negative one right now, if you want.'

'Well?'

Dr Young said, 'I'll stake my professional reputation that you're not pregnant . . . good night.'

He was at the door when he looked back at Quinn and added, 'See you do as you're told and stay in bed tomorrow.'

'You won't know if I don't.'

'Oh, yes, I will.' His eyes wrinkled in another grin. 'I'll be looking in again some time during the afternoon. So behave yourself . . .'

Quinn slept reasonably well. When he awoke just after eight o'clock next morning his headache had gone and he felt considerably better. He also felt hungry.

Mrs Buchanan was adamant about breakfast. '. . . Ye ken fine ye're no supposed tae eat when ye hae a temperature. Lay doon again and haud yer wheesht.'

'But I've got no temperature,' Quinn said. 'And the last thing I had to eat was a sandwich yesterday lunchtime. If you don't feed me I'll get in touch with Oxfam.'

She felt his head and grudgingly admitted that he seemed a lot cooler. '. . . I suppose a wee drap of porridge wouldnae dae ye ony harm . . . wi' a nice cup of tea.'

'Can't I have anything else?'

'Ah'll hae less o' yer cheek. What's wrang wi' porridge?'

'Nothing. I only meant it didn't seem much on its own without some toast, for instance.'

'Weel, that's no what ye said. Ye should learn tae speak decent English.'

'First chance I get,' Quinn said. 'Now can I have a couple of slices of toast?'

Mrs Buchanan said, 'We'll hae tae see aboot that.'

She phoned Piper at a quarter past nine. '. . . Ah've got a message frae Mr Quinn. He asked me tae tell ye he's laid by wi' the flu.'

'I'm sorry to hear it.'

'Oh, Ah wasnae surprised when he cam hame looking like death warmed up. The life he lives he's aye asking for trouble. Has naethin' to eat but sandwiches and beer, gets in at a' oors . . . and that raincoat he wears wouldnae keep a flea warm.'

When she paused for breath, Piper said, 'You're quite right. He certainly doesn't take care of himself. Tell him I hope he's better soon. And thanks for ringing me.'

'Oh, haud on. Ah havnae telt ye the message yet. He wonders if maybe ye'll dae him a favour.'

'If I can,' Piper said.

'Weel, it's like this. He's been meanin' to hae a talk the day wi' a body caud Graham—Mrs Ethel Graham. She's the wife o' that man Mr Quinn was tellin' ye aboot yesterday. Her address is Maryland Avenue, Crouch End, and the name o' the hoose is Elm Haven . . .'

At eleven o'clock that morning Detective-Superintendent Hennant received a call from Leman Street police station in the East Head district. In consequence of what he was told he visited the station and there talked to Inspector Aronson of the detective branch.

Aronson said, '. . . His name's Mick Pavitt. Twenty-three years of age and never done an honest day's work in his life. Got quite a bit of form. Small-time stuff: parcels nicked from unlocked cars; two convictions for walking off with hand luggage at King's Cross while the passenger was booking his ticket; one stealing by finding; six months for stripping tyres and fog lamp off a vehicle parked overnight on waste ground. Last time we brought him in was for being in possession of a stolen car-radio. Promised he'd go straight and got a suspended sentence.'

'More a nuisance than a villain,' Hennant said.

'Yes, sir. Gets a job for a few weeks so he can draw unemployment plus supplementary benefit. When he needs a bit extra because his latest bird has more expensive tastes, he goes looking for a car with valuables temptingly laid out on the rear seat.'

'But, so far as you know, he hasn't stolen any vehicle before?'

'No, sir. It's quite out of his line.'

'Where did you find it?'

'In a lock-up in Christian Street off Commercial Road. The place hasn't been used for months and it's pretty derelict. You could open the door by just giving it a hard pull. That's what some kids did this morning. One of our Panda cars happened to be passing and spotted them clambering all over a nearly-new Hillman saloon.'

'And?'

'He chased the kids away, checked the number and put in a radio call. While I was on my way there—after instructing him to secure the door again—Pavitt arrives, bold as brass, and goes into the lock-up. When I walked in he'd already unscrewed the retaining nuts on the radio.'

'What did he have to say?'

'Denied the whole thing. According to him the lock-up had been open and he'd caught sight of the car as he was going by. Knowing it was likely to get damaged if left there like that, he'd gone inside to see if he could find out the name of the owner.'

'How did he explain his tampering with the radio?'

'Hadn't touched it. Must've been somebody else. He'd only been searching for the owner's name and address. Then he was going to tell the police.'

Superintendent Hennant said, 'Well, after all, it could be true. I think I'd like a quiet word with this model citizen.'

Mick Pavitt wore a polo-necked sweater that had once been grey, a black leather jacket with a broken zip, faded blue jeans. His hair was long and untidy and it kept falling over his eyes.

He looked worried when Hennant pulled a chair up to the other side of the table. Inspector Aronson remained standing at the door of the bare little interrogation-room.

The superintendent introduced himself. Then he asked: 'Suppose you start off by telling me how you got mixed up in this affair?'

Pavitt put his hands in his pockets and tilted the chair back on to its hind legs. He said, 'I've already told my story half a dozen times . . . and I ain't repeating it for nobody.'

Hennant said, 'I can see we're going to get along just fine.' He leaned across the table. 'Let's start the way we mean to go on. First, take your hands out of your pockets. Second, sit up straight. If you loosen the legs of that chair I'll have you charged with malicious damage to police property.'

'I ain't doing nothing wrong,' Pavitt said.

He used one hand to brush the hair out of his eyes. Then very slowly he let the chair down on to its front legs.

'Not now,' Hennant said. 'But don't be tempted to get beyond yourself. I'm mostly a reasonable man . . . except when I have an off day. This is one of them. So watch it,

Mick, just watch it.'

In a sulky voice, Pavitt said, 'I've been here a long time and they keep asking me the same thing over and over again. It ain't fair.'

'That all depends which side of the fence you're on. You happen to be on the wrong side because you put yourself there... nobody else.'

'But I'm going straight now. I told the magistrate—'

'A pack of lies, Mick. He might've believed you—I don't. So don't insult my intelligence. Give me the truth and I may be able to help you.'

'It is the truth... honest to God.'

Superintendent Hennant said, 'I ought to have explained that I've got quite a thing about blasphemy. You're already in trouble up to the neck but—' he leaned across the table again and stuck a rigid forefinger in Pavitt's face—'if you take the Lord's name in vain just once more you'll have every reason to feel sorry for yourself. Do you understand?'

Pavitt's eyes flitted here and there but found no comfort anywhere. He said, 'Yes.'

The superintendent relaxed. He said, 'Good. Now I'm going to ask you what Inspector Aronson has already asked you many times since you were brought in this morning. This time, however, you're going to tell a different story—the true story.'

After an inner struggle, Pavitt said, 'I don't know why there should be all this fuss over a car radio.'

'It's not the radio—it's the car.'

'All right, so it's the car. What makes a car all that important? I ain't never been questioned by a superintendent from Scotland Yard before.'

Hennant said, 'Because you've never faced such a serious charge before.'

'You make it sound—' Pavitt was now afraid—'like I'd robbed the Bank of England.'

'Not quite. But near enough to get you a real long stretch.'

'I—I don't know what you're talking about.'

'No? Then perhaps I'd better spell it out for you. I have

reason to believe that you conspired with others, not yet apprehended, to rob the Jauncey Engineering Company, London N.W.10, of £54,000 on the night of November 4. Furthermore, that you took part in an attack on a factory guard at the Jauncey Company's premises which caused . . .'

Mick Pavitt's mouth had dropped open. His growing pallor and long side-burns now gave him a sickly look.

'. . . which caused grievous bodily harm. When arrested, you were in possession of a motor vehicle that we know was used in the robbery. Although given every opportunity, you have failed to provide a satisfactory explanation.'

Superintendent Hennant clasped both hands behind his head and smiled without humour. He said, 'Those are the facts, Mick. We haven't yet traced your accomplices—perhaps we never will—but we've got you. What do you think of your chances?'

In a dry voice, Pavitt said, 'This is the craziest thing I've ever heard. I ain't done none of these things. I don't know nothing about it.'

'You deny that you were involved in the theft of £54,000 from Jauncey Engineering?'

'Yes . . . yes, I do deny it. I don't even know the place. I ain't never been near it in my life.'

'What about the thieves who pulled off this job? You know them, don't you?'

'No, I don't. Honest, Superintendent, honest to—' The word got stuck halfway.

With a look of numb fascination on his pasty face he stared at Hennant and then turned to Inspector Aronson. No one spoke.

Outside the bare little room there were snatches of conversation . . . the brief ringing of a phone bell . . . footsteps tramping past the door . . . voices overlaid by other voices. Inside the interrogation-room Mick Pavitt sat hunched up and shaking, his eyes filled with desperation.

Once or twice he swallowed and made unintelligible sounds that he seemed unable to control. He was like a man who had lost the power of speech.

Then Hennant asked, 'Well, Mick?'

Pavitt swallowed again. 'You won't believe me. Don't matter what I say, you won't believe me.'

'Are you surprised? With your record do you think you'd get a jury to believe this cock-and-bull story that you were looking for the owner's name and address?'

'No, I—' he struggled to find the right words—'I didn't mean that.'

'Then what did you mean?'

'I meant . . . even if I tell you the real truth.'

'Why not try? For a start, who paid you to hide the car?'

'Nobody. I wasn't mixed up in none of the things you talked about . . . like that factory job and what happened to the guard.'

'You weren't there?'

'No, I didn't have nothing to do with it. I swear I didn't.'

'Don't be so quick to take any oaths,' Hennant said. 'Think of your immortal soul. Where's Harold Graham?'

Pavitt pushed a strand of greasy hair away from his eyes. He said, 'I don't know any Graham. Who is he?'

'Don't you read the papers?'

'Not much. It's a bit out of my line.'

Hennant said, 'Which, I imagine, is more at home with the strip cartoons.'

He unclasped his hands and leaned forward and asked, 'How would you like to begin at the beginning, Mick, and tell me the truth, the whole truth, and nothing but the truth?'

Pavitt's inner conflict lasted only a moment. Then he said in a miserable voice, 'I would—if I thought you'd believe me.'

'You will—without laying down any conditions. Otherwise you won't be in trouble up to the neck; you'll be in it right over your head. This isn't petty theft. This time you've got yourself involved in something so big it'll swallow you whole . . . long dirty hair and all.'

In a tone that crushed the last of Pavitt's spirit, he added, 'I'm the only one who can save you. Without me you haven't a snowball-in-hell chance. Have you got that through your dandruff?'

'Yes—yes, sir.'

'Good. It seems I haven't laboured in vain. Now, are you prepared to admit you were in the act of stealing that car radio when you were arrested?'

'Yes.' Pavitt had his head bent and he was barely audible.

Superintendent Hennant said, 'Look up and speak up . . . That's better. Remember that when I've finished with you, Inspector Aronson has to take it all down in the form of a statement and get you to sign it.'

'I'll sign anything as long as it's true,' Pavitt said.

'It'll be whatever you want it to be. Only you can guarantee whether it's the truth or not. How did the car get into that lock-up in Christian Street?'

'I—I put it there.'

'When?'

'Night before last.'

'That was the night of November 4, wasn't it?'

Pavitt took a little while to work out the date in his head. Then he nodded and said, 'Yes.'

'What time that night?'

'Can't swear to five minutes either way but must've been about half-past ten.'

'That's near enough. How did you come into possession of the car?'

'It was—' Pavitt's eyes were trying to conceal themselves behind his overhanging hair—'it was parked in a street down by the docks . . . and whoever left it there had forgot to lock the door.'

'Some people are very thoughtful,' Hennant said. 'So you nicked it?'

'Yes. I'm not denying what I did because I promised I'd tell you the truth seeing as how you're going—'

'One thing at a time. How did you get the car started?'

'The key was in the ignition.'

'Even more thoughtful. One can only assume that the driver was either very absent-minded or he had somewhere to go in a great hurry. Is that what you thought . . . or didn't you bother thinking about it at all?'

Pavitt shifted uneasily. He looked as though he preferred

to keep his thoughts to himself.

The superintendent said, 'All right, never mind. What was the name of the street where you found the car?'

'St Thomas More Street.'

'Where is that?'

'Runs down to the riverside next to St Katherine Dock.'

Hennant looked up at Inspector Aronson. The inspector said, 'It forms a T-junction with St Katherine's Way to the right and Wapping High Street to the left.'

'And straight ahead lies the river?'

'Yes, sir. If you'd like to see a map—'

'Later, thank you,' Hennant said.

He turned to Pavitt again and asked, 'Whereabouts in St Thomas More Street was the car parked?'

'Down near the foot.'

'Couldn't go much further without falling into the Thames . . . m-m-m?'

Pavitt said, 'No.'

When he got rid of a lump in his throat, he mumbled, 'No, sir.'

'I see. Any other cars parked around that spot?'

'No, it was the only one. Never much doing there at that time of night.'

'But you were there. Why?'

Even more uneasily, Pavitt said, 'Just taking a walk.'

'To get some fresh air in your lungs before going to bed?'

'Something like that . . . sir.'

In a lowering tone, Superintendent Hennant said, 'Fresh air at the dockside . . . taking a walk on a piddling wet night when it was coming down in buckets . . .'

He rested both hands on the table and bent forward threateningly. Then he went on, 'You disappoint me, Mick. I don't mind lies but I also don't suffer fools gladly. I have either to believe everything you tell me—or nothing.'

With a look of desperation, Pavitt said, 'But I've told you the truth about the car . . . and that.'

'How do I know? If you can lie about one thing you may be lying about all the rest. And you weren't taking a late-night walk, were you?'

With his eyes on the table, Pavitt mumbled, 'No.'

'Speak up. Were you or weren't you?'

'No... I wasn't.'

'You were wandering around hoping to find something that had been left unprotected—something you could flog for a few quid. Isn't that it?'

'Yes.'

'And instead you found an unlocked car with the key in the ignition?'

'Yes.'

Hennant said, 'Good. You're doing fine. Go on helping me and I'll try to help you. Apart from the radio, what else of value was in the car?'

Relief showed in Pavitt's eyes. He said, 'Nothing.'

'Wasn't there any luggage? An attaché case, for instance?'

'No, nothing at all.'

'How about the boot?'

'It was locked... and I couldn't open it.'

'Was that partly why you drove the car to that lock-up in Christian Street?'

'Yes.'

'What did you find when you forced the boot?'

'I never touched it. I didn't have time.'

'Why not? It's Friday now and you've had the car hidden away since Wednesday night.'

'Yes... but I stayed away from the lock-up all yesterday. I only went back this morning—' Pavitt fingered the neck of his sweater and became shifty-eyed again—'because I thought it was safe.'

'Famous last words,' Hennant said. He glanced at Aronson. 'Have you had a look inside the boot?'

'Yes, sir. We opened it when the car was brought in.'

'And?'

'Some tools, the spare wheel, an AA member's handbook, a new fan belt in its original carton and top and bottom hoses for the engine. Nothing else, sir.'

'I didn't expect there would be,' Hennant said.

'No, sir. But while we're on the subject of the boot I

should like to discuss a certain matter with you . . . when you've finished questioning Pavitt, of course.'

'I've finished now. He's all yours.'

'Very good, sir. Is it all right if I get someone else to take his statement while I tell you what's on my mind?'

Hennant said, 'By all means.' He got to his feet and stared down at Pavitt. 'Look at me, Mick, and listen carefully. Do you realize how many offences you could be charged with?'

Pavitt swallowed a couple of times. He said, 'Quite a few . . . I suppose.'

'Don't bother to suppose. I'll tell you. For a start, have you got a licence?'

'No.'

'Then here's a rough list. Taking away and driving a motor vehicle without the owner's consent: driving said vehicle on the public highway without a licence: also without third-party insurance: intent to steal various parts and items of equipment from the vehicle: attempted theft of the car radio. That'll do to be going on with although I could think of some more if I tried.'

In a plaintive voice, Pavitt said, 'But you promised to go easy on me if I told you the truth about everything. And I have. Honest, I have.'

'No one made any such promise,' Hennant said. 'However, I did say that if you told the truth I might be able to help you. And I think I can . . . providing you co-operate.'

'Don't reckon that—' Pavitt eased the neck of his sweater —'that I got much choice.'

The superintendent said, 'Not very gracious . . . but then you don't mix in gracious company. If you aren't charged with the other offences will you plead guilty to the attempted theft of the radio?'

'That'll mean I'll do the six months suspended sentence as well as what I'll get for this lot.'

'So you will. But you should've thought of that before you went for a stroll in the rain on Wednesday night. You also forget that you'll be found guilty in any case. However, if you prefer to be charged with everything we can dig up—'

'No . . . no, please. I'll do as you say.'

'It's not what I say. We still have to get the inspector's approval.'

Aronson said, 'That's all right with me, sir. Maybe our young friend here will appreciate leniency and behave himself when he comes out.'

'Maybe,' Hennant said. 'Right now you can have our young friend removed. The wider the generation gap the better . . .'

Someone took Mick Pavitt away. When he had gone, Aronson told Superintendent Hennant about the spare wheel.

'. . . It was wet and muddy, sir. Not much doubt it had been used recently.'

'Such as Wednesday night.'

'And not after that, sir. Since then it's been locked in the boot.'

'True. Anything else?'

'Yes, sir. The tyre was flat.'

Hennant said, 'Nothing strange about that. The question is whether Graham had a puncture before or after he looted the safe.'

'That's the whole point, sir. It wasn't punctured . . . although the effect was the same.'

'Meaning what?'

'The dust cap hadn't been screwed down tight. That's the first thing I noticed when I examined the tyre. After I took the cap off I found that the valve was loose as well. Wouldn't hold any air in at all.'

Superintendent Hennant plucked at his lower lip. Then he asked, 'Are you quite sure there was no puncture?'

'Positive, sir. I had it thoroughly tested several times. First they inflated it with the valve still loose. Soon as they disconnected the compressor all the air rushed out. Then they tightened the valve and blew the tyre up again. It stayed at the correct pressure.'

'What about testing under water?'

'Oh, I watched them do that myself. They immersed the wheel in every position you could think of . . . but not a trace of any bubbles. That tyre was as sound as the day it was made.'

'Interesting . . . very interesting,' Hennant said. 'What conclusions do you draw from all this?'

'Well, sir, tyre valves have been known to work loose. The same thing could happen to a dust cap.'

'But not both together . . . m-m-m?'

Inspector Aronson took a long time to answer. At last, he said, 'The odds against it are greater, sir, but it's still possible. If, on the other hand, it didn't happen accidentally—'

'Then someone let down one of Mister Graham's tyres,' Hennant said. 'We can guess where and when. The big question is—why?'

CHAPTER VII

PIPER DEALT WITH THE MORNING'S CORRESPONDENCE, tape-recorded several letters and disposed of a number of queries. It was almost ten o'clock when he phoned Mrs Ethel Graham.

She had a pleasant voice but she sounded tired. He could understand that the past thirty hours had taken a lot out of her.

'. . . I'm an insurance assessor, Mrs Graham, and I wondered if we might have a chat about what happened at Jauncey Engineering on Wednesday night.'

It would have been awkward if she had questioned his official standing. But she merely said, 'I'm afraid there's nothing I can really tell you. The police have already been here and I couldn't help them at all. You'd only be wasting your time.'

'Well, it's all in the day's work. I've been asked to call . . . and I'd appreciate it very much if you could spare me a few minutes.'

Mrs Graham said indifferently, 'I don't suppose I've any

reason to object. I'll be at home all day so you can choose your own time . . .'

The trees in Maryland Avenue had shed most of their leaves and wind-drift lay banked against the garden wall outside the house called Elm Haven. Rambler roses flanking the concrete drive had lost all but their last few withered petals.

Somewhere in the house Piper could hear soft music. It stopped as soon as he rang the bell. Seconds later the door opened.

She was a small, trim-looking woman with dark hair, dark eyes and an appealing mouth. There were lines of strain around her eyes and Piper got the impression she had not been sleeping very well.

In the same disinterested voice she had used on the phone, she said, 'You're a little earlier than I'd expected . . . but it doesn't matter. Please come in . . .'

He followed her into a comfortably-furnished room with an electric radiator that glowed and flickered like a log fire. The radiants had not been switched on but the room was pleasantly warm.

She asked him if he would like to take his coat off. '. . . In this weather there's less chance of catching cold when you go out.'

Piper said, 'Thank you all the same but I think I'll keep it on. I won't be taking up any more of your time than I can help.'

'Oh, that's all right. Now you're here there's no rush. What did you want to ask me?'

'Well, to start with, has your husband been away from home a lot in recent months?'

'No, but—' the words came out as though they had been carefully rehearsed—'he's been working late at the office far more than he ever used to do.'

'Do you now suspect that this was only an excuse for coming home late?'

Mrs Graham moistened her lips. She said, 'I don't need to suspect—I know. The police have told me he seldom left the factory after six o'clock.'

'Would you have known if he went out of town on those occasions when he returned late?'

'No. How could I?'

'Not very easily,' Piper said. 'Did you ever have any idea that he might be deceiving you?'

She hesitated, her mouth dejected. Then she said, 'No . . . never anything tangible. But in the past few weeks I felt he was . . . well, different somehow. I put it down to the fact that he was working very hard.'

Without emphasis, she added, 'He had also something on his mind that I knew must be depressing him.'

'Had he discussed it with you?'

'Oh, yes, more than once. In fact—' she shook her head and sighed—'I could almost feel he wasn't to blame for what he did. After all, he was only guessing.'

'About what?'

'That he might lose his job when the company was taken over.'

'I didn't know there had been a take-over bid for Jauncey Engineering,' Piper said.

'It's not official yet but everything's settled apart from the actual signing. Of course, people in executive positions like my husband were told the new organization would involve no changes . . . company was to remain autonomous . . . security of employment guaranteed.'

In the same flat tone, she went on, 'I thought he was worrying himself for nothing but he told me, right from the start, that he'd seen it all before. That sort of guaranteee was worthless. No job was safe—from the managing director down to the factory cleaners.'

'So you think it was fear of dismissal that drove him to do it?'

'Oh, I'm quite sure he had no other real motive.'

'How about this woman called Marshall?'

Mrs Graham's face tightened very slightly. She said, 'He didn't want her—not as a woman, I mean. But he couldn't open the safe without the other key. And the only way to get it was to make her his partner.'

'You don't believe she's his mistress?'

'Not for one moment. Oh, there's no doubt he's been deceiving me ever since he began to plan this thing but I'll never believe he was unfaithful. I know him too well for that.'

'You think they'll share the money and then separate?'

'They've probably done that already,' Mrs Graham said.

Piper wondered what Harold Graham would have to do before he destroyed his wife's faith in him. The fact that he was a thief, that the police were hunting for him, meant very little to her. If he went to prison she would wait for him, so long as he had not been unfaithful.

She was watching Piper with a look of apathy on her tired face. Time seemed to have no meaning for her.

He asked, 'If your husband isn't caught, do you think you'll ever see him again?'

'I don't know. Perhaps some day . . .'

'Do you want to?'

'Does that mean—' she sounded as though she were asking for the sake of asking—'you think I shouldn't?'

'It's not for me to judge how you should feel about your husband,' Piper said.

She gave him a sad smile. After a little pause, she said, 'I'm glad you were kind enough to say that. I won't judge him, either. I haven't any right.'

'Why?'

'Because he's never been dishonest in his life. If anyone's to blame it's me.'

'In what way?'

'Somehow I must've let him down. Whatever happened —even the loss of his position with the Company—he'd have faced up to it if I hadn't failed him as a wife.'

'That isn't necessarily true,' Piper said. 'They say every man has his price . . . and £54,000 is a pretty big inducement without any failings on your part.'

'No, I've always understood my husband and I should've realized what this take-over affair was doing to him. I should've seen he was worried for my sake. If he did lose his job we'd have to go without a lot of things we'd been accustomed to . . . and so he had to do something drastic.'

'But leaving you like this isn't going to maintain your standard of living,' Piper said.

She shrugged impatiently. She said, 'I can't hope to explain. I only know he didn't touch our savings . . . and he could've drawn everything out. That shows he didn't desert me because of some other woman, doesn't it? I'll never stop saying it's the Company's fault. They drove him to do what he did . . .'

Without any warning she sat down and put her face in her hands and began to weep. She was crouched in her chair, trembling with grief, when Piper left the room.

He could still hear her as he opened the front door and went out. Very quietly he pulled it shut.

On his way to the double gates he never looked back. He had learned all he was likely to learn from Mrs Ethel Graham.

She blamed herself, she blamed the Company—anyone but her husband. Soon the time would come when she would put all the blame on his mistress. The one thing she would never admit was that he had abandoned her for some other woman.

Perhaps at the back of her mind she would go on hoping that he might get in touch with her some day. If he did . . .

To Piper it was immaterial. Right then she had no idea where her husband had gone when he rifled the firm's safe.

He could appreciate what she had suffered in recent months, the load of worry that she and Harold Graham had carried ever since they learned that Jauncey Engineering was being taken over. No one knew the effect it might have had on their relationship.

Then Graham cracked under the mounting strain. Perhaps there had always been a weakness in his character—a weakness which showed itself when the pressure became too great. Perhaps his wife had nagged at him until he could take her nagging no longer.

There came a time when he had to get away, when the

temptation to start a new life became irresistible. And Yvonne Marshall provided the key . . . in more senses than one.

In Graham's eyes it must have seemed like the prospect of being reborn. He had left his wife whatever savings they possessed because there had been no need to leave her penniless. Fifty-four thousand pounds was enough without stealing from his wife as well as from his employers.

She would go on nursing her illusions long after the rest of the world had forgotten Harold Graham and the theft of Jauncey Engineering Company's payroll . . . or she would make the pretence. As the years went by, even she was bound to recognize the truth about Graham and his mistress.

Piper had a lot of sympathy for Mrs Ethel Graham. In defending her husband she had revealed her own inadequacies.

'. . . Somehow I must've let him down. Whatever happened . . . he'd have faced up to it if I hadn't failed him as a wife.'

She would never live again as a whole person unless Graham was caught. Only then would she learn that he had wanted to get away from her as well as from the pressure of circumstances, that the money had only been the means of escape, that Yvonne Marshall was his real motive.

Quinn had been saved a fruitless journey. If he had visited Crouch End he would have found out nothing useful. Harold Graham had kept his secret well.

There was no hurry to tell Quinn it had been more or less a waste of time. After he got over his bout of flu and was back at work would be soon enough.

Meanwhile the police were pursuing their inquiries. If they failed to discover Graham's whereabouts, no one else stood any real chance.

International Rentacars phoned Scotland Yard just before lunchtime. They were put through to Detective-Sergeant Freeson who told them Superintendent Hennant was out and would not be back until one o'clock.

'. . . If you'd like to give me some idea what it's about . . .'

'Well, one of the morning papers has a report on that robbery the night before last—the affair at some factory near the North Circular Road. Know the one I mean?'

Freeson said, 'Yes, I do. It was the theft of £54,000 from the Jauncey Engineering Company.'

'That's right. Your switchboard says Detective-Superintendent Hennant is in charge of the case and if we have any information we should give it to him.'

'In his absence you can give it to me,' Freeson said. 'I'll see he gets it soon as he comes in.'

'Wouldn't it be better if I spoke to him personally?'

'No . . . but that's up to you. Give me your number and I'll ask him to ring you.'

The man at the other end said, 'Wouldn't be much good, I'm afraid, if it's after one. I'll be out at lunch. To save delay, maybe I'd better tell you.'

'Maybe you'd better,' Freeson said.

'All right. Well, it's like this: a week ago last Wednesday —that was October 28—we supplied a car to somebody who could be one of the people you're interested in. According to what I read it seems more than likely.'

'Which one?'

'The woman. In the paper it says her name's Mrs Marshall—Yvonne Marshall. You're after her as well as that fellow Graham, aren't you?'

Sergeant Freeson said, 'At the moment, let's say they're wanted for questioning.'

'Oh, yes, of course. Anyway, this woman hired a car for two weeks, commencing November 4. Said she'd pick it up between twelve and two. When she signed the hire application form she used the name Yvonne Marshall and gave her home address as 19 Brinton Drive, Dollis Hill, N.W.2. Must be the same person, mustn't it?'

'Well, that's our Mrs Marshall's address, all right. The details tallied with her driving licence, I suppose?'

'Naturally. The licence is always checked to make sure it's in order. And the signature on her licence was in the same handwriting as the name she wrote on our application form. I have a copy of it in front of me right now.'

'Does any member of your staff remember what this woman looked like?'

'Yes, you're in luck there. As it happens, the young lady who filled in the customer's details also attended to her when she called here the day before yesterday to collect the car. Her description matches the one in this morning's paper.'

'You've been most helpful,' Freeson said. 'May I have the make, colour and registration number of the vehicle that Mrs Marshall hired from you?'

'Oh, sure. It was a Ford Cortina: pale green: registration number . . .'

He also provided the sergeant with engine and chassis serial numbers and speedometer mileage recorded before the car left International's premises. In addition he promised that the young lady would be available when someone from Scotland Yard called to get a statement from her.

Then he said, 'There's one thing more that just might be significant.'

Sergeant Freeson said, 'Go ahead, sir. The superintendent will be grateful for any help you can give.'

'Well, this might not mean anything but I feel I should mention it. Apparently Mrs Marshall—if it was Mrs Marshall—was told the car had a full tank of petrol. It's our standard practice, as perhaps you know, to fill up each vehicle before it leaves . . .'

'Yes, I'm aware of that,' Freeson said.

'I thought you might be. However, to cut a long story short, she asked how far a tankful would take her and one of the staff said she should be able to do well over two hundred miles. At that, Mrs Marshall said something to the effect that she could always fill up later.'

'Didn't mention which direction she was taking, did she?'

'Unfortunately, no.'

'I'm not surprised. It would be expecting too much. The lady is no fool.'

'Nevertheless, it would seem she had a pretty long journey ahead of her.'

'Or that's what she wanted you to think,' Freeson said.

Superintendent Hennant got back just after one o'clock. When he had heard the story of the hired car, he said, 'Looks to me, Sergeant, that they needed two cars because Graham was dumping his Hillman in St Thomas More Street and he needed Mrs Marshall to take him wherever they were going.'

'Why should both of them go all that way, sir, to get rid of the Hillman when they could've left it anywhere?'

'That's what I've been turning over in my mind since I left Leman Street. And the only answer is that anywhere wouldn't have served their purpose. By leaving the car where it was found, Graham has given us a nice little job to do . . . with no guarantee that it won't be a complete waste of time and effort.'

Freeson said, 'We'll have to check all vessels that sailed from the docks on, or since, Wednesday night, sir. There is just a chance that he and the Marshall woman have skipped the country.'

'Then why two cars? The Hillman could've taken both them and the eight attaché cases . . . if they'd booked passage on some ship or other.'

'You think, sir, the whole idea was to lay a false trail?'

Superintendent Hennant said, 'Thinking won't get us anywhere, Sergeant. We need facts. And I'd give a lot to know one thing. What happened to the pale green Ford Cortina that Mrs Yvonne Marshall hired?'

CHAPTER VIII

QUINN STAYED IN BED all Friday. In the afternoon Dr Young called, took his temperature, sounded his chest and told him he was on the mend.

'Your pipes are still a bit wheezy but that's from smoking . . . and if you want to kill yourself it's your own business.'

'Thanks,' Quinn said. 'Your bedside manner may not be good but at least it's original.'

'My patients benefit more from the truth than they do from the finest bedside manner.'

'You should hang that up in your surgery as a Thought for—' Quinn had a bout of coughing that left him breathless.

When he got his wind back, he asked, 'Where was I?'

Dr Young said, 'From the sound of you I'd say halfway to the cemetery. If you had any sense you'd stop indoors over the weekend. But if you had any sense you wouldn't need my advice.'

'If I had any sense I'd apply to be put on some other doctor's list.'

'It works both ways,' Young said. 'Don't tempt me. Good afternoon . . .'

Friday evening's papers reported the finding of Harold Graham's car near St Katherine Dock. A Scotland Yard spokesman also stated that information had been received regarding a second car used in the robbery at Jauncey Engineering Company's works.

> It is now known that a woman believed to be Mrs Yvonne Marshall hired a pale green Ford Cortina from a rentacar firm on Wednesday, November 4. All police forces, garages and filling stations are asked to be on the lookout for this vehicle which bears the registration number LQB 898 J.
>
> Any member of the public who may have knowledge of a car bearing this number is asked to get in touch with New Scotland Yard, Tel. No. 01-855-1212 or any police station.

Saturday's *Morning Post* published the latest developments along with a half-column rehash of the Jauncey Payroll Theft. Most of it had been taken from the story Quinn had phoned in from a call box in Crouch End on Thursday afternoon.

He read it and re-read it while he was having his porridge, toast and tea in bed. When Mrs Buchanan came upstairs to collect his breakfast dishes she found he was up and dressed.

She closed the door and settled her back against it. She asked, 'And whaur d'ye think ye're gaun?'

Quinn said, 'Look, Mrs B. I can't stay in bed indefinitely. You've been like a mother to me and I'm really grateful but—'

'Gie me nane o' yer fancy talk. Ah'm no yer mither and Ah'm no gaun tae be treated like yer mither. The doctor says ye havenae tae stir oot the day and so ye'll bide in the hoose or Ah'll no be responsible.'

'That's all right. I'm not asking you to be responsible.'

'Until ye gang doon wi' the flu again . . . and ye will, as sure as toffee apples. And aw yer gift o' the gab willnae help ye then. 'Cos next time ye're laid by it'll be in the hospital. Ah'll no be carrying yer meals up and doon the stairs.'

'You won't have to,' Quinn said. 'I'm feeling OK now.'

'Oh, ye are, are ye? Then who was it Ah heard barking like a dog? D'ye think maybe Ah'm hearin' things that are no there? Or is it that Ah've gaun daft awthegither? Is that whit ye're sayin'?'

'All right, all right.' He sat down and began unfastening his shoelaces. 'I know when I'm licked. For the rest of today I won't budge out of your wee but and ben.'

'Ye've nae need tae dae me ony favours. Ye're aw the same . . . nane o' ye hae ony consideration for ither folk.'

In the same tone, she asked, 'Whit was wrang wi' the porridge?'

'Nothing. I just couldn't finish it all. You gave me a little too much.'

'Ye had nae mair than ye had yesterday.'

'Well, maybe I wasn't so hungry this morning.'

Mrs Buchanan looked at him. Mrs Buchanan sniffed. Then she collected his breakfast dishes and stacked them on a tray with much ostentatious clatter.

As she went out he heard her grumbling '. . . Hauf the

world's starving and he's got the cheek tae say he had too much. Some folks are too weel aff . . . that's the trouble nooadays . . .'

He phoned Piper's office later that morning and learned the result of his interview with Mrs Graham. In return he told Piper about Miss Field's dislike of her brother-in-law and the suspicions she had harboured for many months.

'. . . They may be sisters but one will say nothing bad about him and the other one nothing good.'

'His wife's protecting her dignity more than her husband,' Piper said. 'That's what it amounts to. I'm afraid my visit to Crouch End didn't achieve very much . . . and neither did yours.'

Quinn said, 'Oh, I don't know. They've provided me with background and atmosphere. Harold Graham's a real person now and not just a name.'

'But that won't help you find him.'

'I never expected I would. Just because I had airy-fairy ideas of what I could do with a five thousand quid reward doesn't mean I fancied my chances of earning it. A good story is the limit of my ambition.'

'So your policy is that the shoemaker should stick to his last,' Piper said.

'Yes. I've learned that it pays off most times. The secret of failure is to let your ambition outstrip your ability. However . . . Thanks for calling on Mrs Graham for me.'

'It's my pleasure.'

Quinn said, 'That's what the bishop said to the actress. Be seeing you . . .'

He went back up to his room, stretched out on the bed and lay thinking about a pale green Ford Cortina that Mrs Yvonne Marshall had hired on Wednesday, November 4. Wherever she meant to go she would want to get rid of the car as soon as possible.

Neither she nor Harold Graham could know how long it would be before the Cortina was traced to her. If the theft at Jauncey Engineering had been discovered before the next day's papers went to press the story would have been on millions of breakfast tables Thursday morning. And among those millions of readers were the people who worked for the rentacar firm.

As Quinn saw it, Graham and Marshall could be sure of little more than twelve hours in which to use the car and then dispose of it. Any longer than that would be a gamble. And a couple who had planned as carefully as they had done were not the type to gamble with £54,000.

Any time after the rentacar firm opened for business on Thursday morning, the whole scheme was at risk if they had not abandoned the car. They had to reckon that its make, colour and registration number would be known the length and breadth of the country within an hour or less.

They could have carried several spare cans of petrol so as to avoid any need to stop at a filling station. Customers were few during the night and an attendant might remember a man and a woman in a pale green Cortina. It would be enough to give the police some kind of lead to follow.

But ample fuel would be no guarantee of success. Time was the critical factor. They had to dump both cars and get to their hiding-place within twelve hours.

At that point Quinn's thoughts were blocked by a question to which there was no immediate answer. It might not have been Graham's car that was abandoned first. If not . . .

. . . *Suppose they got rid of the Cortina and then drove down to St Katherine Dock? That means the Ford can't have got very far . . . which isn't important. What is crucial is that the trail ends at the riverside. But, if so, why bother with the other cars at all? It must've served some purpose. And the obvious one is that they used it to stage their getaway . . .*

Perhaps too obvious. When the police found the pale green Cortina they might not know where the thieves then were but, to some extent, it would prove where Graham and Mrs Marshall had been, the direction they had taken when they left London. And that seemed an unnecessary weakness in a well-planned crime.

. . . Unless they didn't leave London. So it would make no difference where they dumped either car . . . or in which order. Could be that LQB 898 J is right here in town . . . and so are the love-birds. If not, they wouldn't set off on foot. Therefore they've gone for a long sea voyage . . .

Until the Cortina was found, conjecture would only lead to more conjecture. Graham and Yvonne Marshall had now had three days' start. They would hardly be worried about the two cars.

One thing still kept nagging at Quinn's mind. The pale green Cortina should have come to light by this time unless it had been deliberately hidden. And there seemed no logical reason why they should have hidden it. Once the car had served its purpose it could have been left anywhere.

. . . The further away the better, of course. But far and near in a town this size are relative terms. Nobody knows the man in the next street . . . or on the next floor in a multi-storey block of flats . . .

Quinn told himself there were too many answers from which to choose. Someone must know where the car had been left between Wednesday night and Thursday morning . . . someone must know . . . someone . . . someone . . .

Ideas revolved sluggishly in his head and thinking became difficult. While he was trying to find his way through to the beginning he fell asleep.

It was Mrs Buchanan who wakened him. She said, 'It's a mite early for yer dinner but Ah've got a nice wee drap o' soup on the stove and Ah thought maybe ye'd fancy some. Be a change from a' them sandwiches ye're aye ha'in and should help ye get yer strength back.'

'I don't know what I'd do without you,' Quinn said. 'How about you and me getting married?'

'Aw, awa' wi' ye, man. Ye're aye talkin' daft. Whaur will ye hae yer soup—up here or ben the kitchen?'

'The kitchen every time. It's more intimate.'

She shook her head at him. She said, 'That's no way to talk to a body auld enough to be yer mither. Mind ye—' a momentary look of kindness showed in her eyes but her voice was as gruff as ever—'if Ah had been yer mither

Ah'd have seen ye were drooned at birth . . .'

Detective-Superintendent Hennant received a teleprint message from Interpol at eleven-thirty Saturday morning. It told him there was no trace of either Harold Graham or Mrs Yvonne Marshall. Their descriptions had been circulated on the Continent and a watch was being maintained.

'Not much hope in that direction after three days,' Sergeant Freeson said. 'In my opinion, sir, it's like looking for a needle in a haystack.'

'Especially when the odds are it's the wrong haystack,' Hennant said.

He had a meeting with the AC and returned to his room shortly before noon. A couple of minutes later the switchboard put through a call from the Neptune Garage in Abbey Road, St John's Wood.

'. . . Not much doubt it's the same car. Been here all the time. I've given instructions it hasn't to be touched.'

'Have someone keep an eye on it,' Hennant said. 'I'll be with you as quickly as traffic will allow.'

He got there with Sergeant Freeson at twenty past twelve. A man called Beech was waiting for them in the ground-floor office.

Beech said, 'She phoned some time last Monday and asked if she could have her car serviced and a damaged wing beaten out and resprayed. Told Reception she'd bring it in Wednesday afternoon or evening and wouldn't want it before the eighteenth as she was going abroad for two weeks.'

'When did she bring it in?'

'About eight o'clock Wednesday night. Explained to the attendant that she'd arranged for an engine overhaul and he told her to run the car down to our underground car-park. Made a note of her name and details of the car and passed the chit to Reception next morning.'

'What name did she use?'

'Same name she'd given when she phoned on Monday—Mrs. Whitelaw.'

'Any address?'

'No. We don't ask for the address when the customer hasn't an account. She'd have paid cash when she collected the car.'

'How is it you didn't discover it was the one we're looking for until today if it's been on your premises since Wednesday night?'

'We've got two hundred vehicles in our underground carpark,' Beech said. 'Nobody goes round inspecting the registration numbers. This Mrs Whitelaw was in no hurry so I left it for a few days. It was only this morning when I started making out the work schedule for Monday that something about the number of her car struck me as being familiar. Then I rang Scotland Yard.'

Superintendent Hennant said, 'I'm grateful for what you've done. I wish more people had your memory as well as your sense of duty. Now I'd like to see the car that was left by someone calling herself Mrs Whitelaw.'

It was a pale green Ford Cortina with mud-spattered doors and radiator grille. Rain marks had dried on windscreen and rear window. The licence disc and the registration plates bore the number LQB 898 J.

The fuel indicator showed that the tank was full. The speedometer registered 7414 miles.

When Hennant had made a note of the mileage, Beech said, 'The attendant who was on duty Wednesday night doesn't get here until seven o'clock this evening . . . but I sent someone round to his house soon as I spotted the number of the car.'

'And?'

'He remembers the young woman who was driving this Cortina. From his description of her she's the one you're looking for. I've told him to get here toot-sweet because you'll want a statement from him.'

'You did right,' Hennant said. 'Sergeant Freeson will take the statement. I'm leaving him to keep watch on the car until it's been taken away . . .'

Engine and chassis serial numbers tallied with International

Rentacars records. A representative of the company certified that the car was one of their fleet of vehicles, that it had been rented to a woman in possession of a driving licence issued to Mrs Yvonne Marshall, and that she had signed the rental form in this name.

The mileage recorded when she took delivery was 7399. The figure on the clock when noted by Superintendent Hennant was 7414.

He said, 'That means she travelled a total distance of roughly fifteen miles. Let's see how far it is from A to B and then to C.'

Sergeant Freeson laid a ruler against the wall map of London and suburbs and measured the entire journey. After he had done some mental arithmetic, he said, 'It's all very approximate, of course, sir, but I make the round trip as follows: International Rentacars depot in Knightsbridge—Jauncey Engineering—St Katherine Dock—Neptune Garage in Abbey Road. That's a total of twenty-two miles.'

'Yet, according to the speedometer, she did only fifteen miles,' Hennant said. 'I'd better measure it and you watch to see I don't make any mistakes.'

Both distances agreed. If Mrs Marshall had driven the route Knightsbridge—North Circular Road—St Katherine Dock—St John's Wood she would have covered twenty-two miles.

They re-checked their figures but the answer was still the same. If the clock on the car was correct they had a discrepancy of seven miles.

Superintendent Hennant said, 'No use blaming the speedometer. The fault is in our reasoning. We know she collected the car from the depot in Knightsbridge: we also know she got rid of it at the Neptune Garage in Abbey Road, St John's Wood. Those are facts. But the bit in the middle is conjecture which must be faulty.'

'Not altogether, sir,' Freeson said. 'The night patrolman at Jauncey Engineering saw two cars outside the Administration building. One of them is bound to have been this Ford Cortina. You don't think there were three cars involved, do you, sir?'

'No. That way lies insanity. All I'm suggesting is that Mrs Marshall didn't go to St Katherine Dock when she drove out of the factory.'

Sergeant Freeson studied the wall map again. He said, 'Since it was Yvonne Marshall who hired the car and Yvonne Marshall who disposed of it when the job was over, we're entitled to assume it was Yvonne Marshall who drove the car to this unknown place that made the total distance add up to fifteen miles . . . aren't we, sir?'

'I'll give you permission to make that assumption,' Hennant said.

'Well, sir, there's only one place she could've gone.'

'And where is that, Sergeant?'

'I don't know, sir. I mean I don't know its location. But I'm willing to bet it's the spot they chose to hide the stolen money.'

Superintendent Hennant said, 'I wouldn't take your bet, Sergeant, if you offered me odds of a thousand to one. But while you're in this bright mood perhaps you'd tell me if Mrs Marshall went back to the hiding-place after she got rid of the Cortina or if you think she went somewhere else.'

'Well, if I were asked to make a guess, sir . . .'

The lines around Hennant's sharp blue eyes deepened in a smile. He said, 'As they're so fond of saying on television these days, Sergeant, be my guest.'

'Very good, sir. I'd say it's pretty obvious she made her way somewhere to wait for Graham?'

'And left the fifty-four thousand pounds hidden in the other place?'

'Yes, sir.'

'As an insurance against the risk of being picked up?'

'Something like that, sir.'

'If they did, then they won't have left the country,' Hennant said.

Sergeant Freeson hunched his thick shoulders. He had a barrel chest and he carried himself as though he had put on his jacket without removing the coat hanger.

He said, 'I never thought there was much in that theory, sir. Leaving the Hillman on the dockside seemed just too obvious. If they'd meant to sneak away on some tramp steamer one car would've been enough. They wouldn't have needed to go through all that rigmarole with the rentacar firm and the garage in Abbey Road.'

Hennant said, 'You've got a logical mind, Sergeant. I'm inclined to agree that the money is somewhere in the London area . . . although Graham and Marshall may have gone much further afield. The question is what they're living on and how long it'll last.'

'I'm not sure, sir—' Freeson glanced at the wall map—'that it would be better if we asked ourselves what Graham's living on.'

'Meaning that he and the Marshall woman didn't join up after they got rid of the two cars?'

'Something like that, sir.'

'Quinn of the *Morning Post* had some such idea,' Hennant said. 'He suggested that she double-crossed Graham once she had her hands on the money. Are you coming round to his way of thinking?'

'Well, he could be right, sir. I keep remembering what Inspector Aronson told you about the spare wheel in Graham's car—the tyre was flat although it hadn't a puncture. You wondered why anyone should've unscrewed the valve. Adding up what we've now learned, Quinn's suggestion provides a reason.'

Superintendent Hennant walked round to the other side of the desk and lowered himself slowly into his chair. With a smile crinkling his eyes, he said, 'It's plausible, Sergeant, plausible to a degree. I'm not disposed to reject it until I have something better to put in its place. If it was Mrs Marshall who tampered with the valve of that tyre . . .'

'Then she must've wanted Graham to be delayed changing the wheel so that he wouldn't leave the factory at the same time as she did.'

'Yes, Sergeant. That's how it looks . . . on the surface. But what difference did it make whether he was delayed or not? They weren't taking the same route. He was going down to the docks while she planted the stolen money and then got rid of her hired car.'

Freeson nodded and said, 'I've been puzzled about that, too, sir. I can only suggest they hadn't intended to separate when they left the factory but the flat tyre necessitated a change of plan.'

'No, that won't wash, either. The use of two cars means they had two different tasks to perform. I'm not saying she didn't trick Graham in the end but she could've done that without letting down one of his tyres.'

'Very true, sir. I know I'm arguing against myself . . . but there's also the timetable to be taken into account. Doesn't really matter when Graham got away from the factory. What we can reckon is that it must've been not far off seven when Mrs Marshall left and—'

'—and she'd got to the Neptune Garage by eight o'clock after making a call somewhere en route,' Hennant said. 'The question we have to ask is why she chose that particular garage.'

'Seems obvious to me, sir. It was conveniently situated. Not too far to travel after she'd planted the money—'

'—yet not too near the place where she was going to lie low,' Hennant said.

Sergeant Freeson hunched his shoulders again. He said, 'I've changed my mind about that, sir. I think they're one and the same place. Can't believe she'd let those eight cases out of her sight.'

'Nor can I, Sergeant, nor can I.'

The superintendent plucked at his lower lip. Then he added, 'But we're still stuck with the flat tyre. Right from the start I knew where it had happened and when. Now I'm pretty sure who was responsible. But I'm no nearer answering my original question—why?'

CHAPTER IX

Mrs Buchanan allowed Quinn to go out on Sunday morning. Before he left he had to promise he would be back in time for a hot dinner.

'... Mind what Ah'm saying noo. See ye're hame sharp. Ah'll no hae ye wasting a guid meal.'

The wind had dropped and it was a cold still day with traces of mist. He wrapped his scarf twice round his neck and set off at a brisk walk.

It felt good to be mobile again after being cooped up indoors for what seemed more than a couple of days. If there had been time he would have walked all the way. Instead he caught a train to Holborn, changed there for Aldwych and completed his journey on foot.

When he got to the *Morning Post* building it was just half-past nine. Hardly anyone else had arrived. With a feeling of virtue he typed a note and left it in Features.

> Sorry to disappoint but you can cancel the order for flowers and tell them not to set up my obit. When you see He-Who-Must-Be-Obeyed say I've gone to Jauncey Engineering. This is supposed to be my day off but I'm a martyr to duty.
>
> PS. Mention that I've borrowed one of the company cars.
>
> PPS. Also borrowed one of your cigarettes. Regret to see you've gone on to a cheaper brand. If you've found that smoking has become too expensive you should give it up. I speak as a friend.

Jauncey Engineering Company was on the right-hand side of the North Circular Road between Harrow Road and Grand Union Canal. He slowed down as he approached the main gates and cruised at a walking pace towards Bransby Lane.

The gates were shut and secured by a padlock and chain at head-height and ground-level. On the right stood a long, glass-roofed building with wire-meshed windows. On the left were the foundations of a new construction surrounded by girders, stacks of bricks, a cement-mixer, mounds of sand and gravel. A partly-finished stretch of roadway ran between the new foundations and a single-storey building further to the left.

Tall production-shops lay on the other side of a centre road running the entire length of the factory from a car-park at one end to a set of gates at Bransby Lane. The whole site was surrounded by a steel-meshed fence on concrete posts and topped with multiple strands of barbed wire sloping outwards.

Quinn told himself Jauncey Engineering had made sure it would be difficult for anyone to get in. What they had not reckoned on was that thieves were already on the inside and had only to get out.

... Chose the right night for it. Pitch-dark and pouring rain. If that fellow Tugwell hadn't turned up at the wrong time the love-birds would've been over the hill and far away long before the theft was discovered. Nice neat job carried out nice and neatly. No violence and no excitement—until Reg Tugwell threw a spanner in the works ...

Bransby Lane gates also were chained and padlocked. Just inside the gates stood a concrete building with a sign above the door: *Security Office.*

It was exactly ten o'clock when Quinn stopped the car and got out. He wondered if the patrolmen worked their usual hours on a Sunday or if he would have to wait until the man on duty finished his round and came back to Security.

... Might be a long wait. Never thought of that. Took it for granted he'd do an hourly patrol and be back here on the hour. Not that I could've done much about it either way. Suppose I could ring to let him know somebody's out-

side but he won't be pleased if he's at the other end of the factory . . .

There was a bell-push on one of the gate-posts. While Quinn was trying to make up his mind he saw a man coming down the first avenue on the left—a tarmac road running between a stretch of well-kept lawn and a building with three or four steps leading up to the wide entrance.

He was a tall, lean man with a stoop that reduced his height. He had overhanging eyebrows and craggy features and a look that said it had been years since he last smiled.

When he caught sight of Quinn, he called out, 'Yes? What're you after?'

Quinn said, 'I was hoping I'd see Reg Tugwell.'

'Oh, were you?'

The man with the hunched back came closer to the gates. His eyes were suspicious.

He asked, 'What made you think you'd find Tugwell here at this time?'

'Someone told me he finished his shift about ten o'clock . . . and it's just ten now.'

'Well, someone told you wrong. Change of shift was an hour ago. What did you want him for?'

'I've got a few quid for him,' Quinn said.

'Have you now?' The thin man pulled down the corners of his mouth. 'Don't tell me old Reg has won the pools.'

'No, nothing like that. I was going to offer him a fiver if he'd talk to me about that affair the other night.'

'What affair?'

'The robbery, of course. How often does somebody walk out of this place with fifty-four thousand nicker?'

The thin man shifted from one foot to the other. With something behind the suspicion in his eyes, he said, 'You don't need to pay Tugwell if you want to know about that. You can read all about it in the papers.'

'I'm one of the fellows who put it in the papers,' Quinn said.

'Oh, I thought as much. We've had one or two of your kind sniffing around here. They asked if they could take a look round the factory but the works manager wouldn't let them step inside the gate.'

Quinn said, 'I'm different. I can see all I need to see from outside. The thing I'm after is a first-hand account of what took place Wednesday night.'

'And you're willing to pay five pounds for that?'

'Sure. If I can't get hold of Tugwell I'll be satisfied with his mate, Ryan. He's the one who called the police, isn't he?'

'Yes. But neither Tugwell nor Ryan know any more—' Resentment had taken the place of suspicion in the thin man's eyes—'any more than I do. I got the whole story when I came on duty at nine o'clock next morning. What's more, I was here when she drove in with that hired car at lunch-time on Wednesday.'

'You're referring to Mrs Marshall?'

'That I am. And I saw her bring the Cortina and park it outside Admin when the rest of the staff had gone home. I was collecting the clock-cards at the time.'

'Interesting,' Quinn said. 'You must be Alfie Platt.'

'That's me. If you want the inside story of what happened I can give it to you.'

'Ah, but you weren't directly involved. After all, it was Tugwell who got bashed over the head and Ryan who sent for the police. You only saw Mrs Marshall put her car outside Admin.'

Platt come closer still. With his face almost touching the bars of the gate, he said, 'Oh, no, that wasn't all I saw. Before Reg Tugwell came back from patrol just after six, Graham drove up from the car-park to Admin. He passed the other car—the green one—and went on to the top of First Avenue so he could turn round and be facing the right way . . .'

In the same breath, Platt added, '. . . and that's all I'm telling you for nothing. If it's worth listening to it's worth paying for.'

Quinn said, 'All right, I'll do a deal with you. Three quid even if you can't tell me anything I don't already know:

five quid if you come up with something new.'

'Who's to say it's new or not?'

'I'll decide that.'

'Which means I'll have to take your word for it.'

'Every man has his price,' Quinn said. 'But mine is higher than a couple of pounds. You can trust me.'

After a struggle with himself, Platt said, 'OK. If you twist me I'll make trouble for you with your boss. What's the name of the paper you work for?'

'*Morning Post*. And now we've settled the financial details can we go some place where there's a bit of warmth? I've just had flu and I don't want to catch pneumonia.'

Platt said, 'No. My orders are to let no one inside the works unless he's got the right authority. And you haven't any. So either we talk like this through the gate or you can keep your money.'

'All right. Now start talking.'

'Not yet. I want your promise you won't mention my name. The firm wouldn't like it.'

'You have my promise,' Quinn said. 'Before I freeze to death let's hear what happened on Wednesday night.'

'Where do you want me to start?'

'The place where you left off. Graham had driven up to the top of First Avenue so he could turn his car round.'

'Oh, yes. Well, he drove back to the Admin entrance and pulled up behind that green Cortina. When he got out he walked round to the front of his own car and stood there for a few seconds.'

'What was he doing?'

'Couldn't say. He was bent down all the time. But I know he must've been examining something at the back of the green car.'

'How do you know that?'

'Because he was facing that way when he stood up again.'

'Where were you?'

'In the Security Office. From the door you can see straight up First Avenue.'

'Could he see you?'

'No. I hadn't switched the light on.'

'Did you think at the time that his behaviour was suspicious?'

Platt wiped a knobbly hand over his face. He said, 'No. Why should I? Graham was one of the bosses. It's not my place to have any opinions on what they do.'

'Your philosophy wouldn't please my Uncle Mao,' Quinn said. 'But never mind. What did Graham do after that?'

'Went into—' Alfie Platt jerked a thumb over his shoulder at the Administration block—'into the offices.'

'And you never saw him again?'

'No. I went home at ten past six. When Reg finished his round he told me Mrs Marshall and the head cashier were working late. I remember wondering why they'd bothered to bring both cars from the car-park ... but it was none of my business, anyway, although it would've been more sensible if they'd finished the work they were doing and then went to the car-park when it was time to go home.'

'Now you know the reason they didn't,' Quinn said.

'Yeah. Who'd have thought a man in Graham's position would turn out to be a wrong 'un?'

'Quite a few people are asking themselves the same question. Did you tell the police what you'd seen Graham doing?'

'No.'

'Why not?'

'They never sent for me. They were too busy interviewing Vic Ryan and Tugwell. Besides, the less I have to do with coppers the better.'

In a sour voice, Platt added, 'I'm not like Reg Tugwell.'

'You mean he's a pal of the busies?'

'Anybody'd think so. He couldn't stop talking about it. And the fuss he's made because he got a knock on the head you'd imagine he'd been in a coma for weeks.'

'Well, he was unconscious,' Quinn said.

'Maybe so. But it couldn't have lasted long. The hospital gave him an X-ray and all they found was a lump on his head. When I was boxing for my unit in the army I got knocked out a couple of times and I got over it soon enough.

There was no going off sick for me.'

'How long was Tugwell off?'

'Until we started the new shift-rota last night. He's now on one a.m. to nine a.m. . . . that's if he turns up again. And I wouldn't like to bet on it.'

'What makes you say that?'

'Because of the way he keeps bellyaching about his nerves and the pains in his head and how he's scared of being alone in the factory at night after what happened.'

'Can't say I blame him,' Quinn said.

A scowl darkened Platt's craggy face. He said, 'If you was on a medical board you'd see through him all right. What he's after is compen. And all this talk about giving up his job is to make sure he gets it. If the fiddle comes off he'll get sick pay for the next six months and a tidy sum of money on top of that.'

'You think it is a fiddle?'

'I'm damn sure of it! He's as fit as you or me. Never imagined he was the kind to go in for swinging the lead. You wouldn't believe the change that's come over him since Wednesday night.'

'That makes three people who have shown up in their true colours,' Quinn said.

A stray thought passed through his mind and was gone— a notion without any real substance. It was too bizarre for serious consideration.

Alfie Platt asked, 'Anything else you want to know?'

'Yes . . . a helluva lot of things I wish you could tell me.'

'Such as what? You must've heard already how Ryan found these gates unlocked when he arrived to take over that night. He smashed a window in the Security Office and rang for the police and they found Tugwell tied up in Mrs Marshall's room in Wages Department . . . and that's about all.'

'Except for one small detail—an empty safe,' Quinn said.

'Well, you don't expect me to know where the money is, do you? Wish I did. I could do a lot with that reward. It would make Tugwell's compensation look damn silly . . .'

Platt poked a hand through the bars of the gate and

rubbed finger and thumb together. In a wheedling tone, he said, 'Talking about money, isn't it about time I saw the colour of yours?'

Quinn said, 'Don't worry. You'll get paid. The more you tell me the more you'll earn.'

'But I don't know any more.'

'You might not think so. For instance, you can explain the procedure you follow with the keys to various places in the factory.'

'What if I can? It won't get you anywhere.'

'That remains to be seen. When you're making your rounds do you carry all the keys with you?'

'All of them except those for the gates.'

'Both North Circular Road and Bransby Lane . . . this one here?'

'Yes. They're the only two ways of getting out of the works.'

'And the keys to both gates are kept in the Security Office?'

'That's right.'

'So to get at them Graham took the office key from Tugwell after he'd hit him over the head?'

Alfie Platt said testily, 'You keep going all round the houses. How else d'you think he opened the gates?'

'I was only asking. This won't take long if you'll just be patient. When Ryan arrived at one a.m. he found these gates unlocked, didn't he?'

'Yes.'

'What about the door of the Security Office?'

'It was locked. Why else d'you think he had to break a window.'

'You've got a point there,' Quinn said. 'But doesn't it seem strange that he took the trouble to relock the door that nobody could see from outside the factory and yet he didn't bother with these gates although he must've known some passers-by might notice that something was wrong and raise the alarm?'

Platt wiped a coarse hand over his face again. He said, 'I don't see nothing strange in it. He didn't padlock the gates when he left because he was in too damned much of a hurry.'

'Yet he took time to lock the Security Office.'

'So what? His car and that green Cortina weren't outside in Bransby Lane then. It was only when he and his woman were out in the open that they wanted to get away before people began wondering what was going on.'

'Maybe. But they shut the gates even if they didn't padlock them.'

'Only because the balloon would've gone up in no time at all if they hadn't. Coppers aren't blind, you know. There's always a patrol car touring the neighbourhood most nights. Do you think they'd have driven past if they'd spotted the gates wide open?'

'You're right,' Quinn said. 'Just one more question . . .'

'See it's the last. I'm already late for my ten o'clock round.'

'This won't take a moment. What happened to the keys for these gates and the Security Office?'

In a crusty voice, Platt said, 'You're not the only one who'd like to know that. They haven't been seen since Wednesday night. We've had a new lock fitted to the door of Security and new padlocks on both gates. Anything else?'

'No, thanks. That's all for now. You can get on with your job.'

'Not before I'm paid. How much are you giving me?'

'I'll leave that to you. What do you think it's worth?'

'Well, you promised me three quid . . . at least. And I've told you the same as Reg Tugwell would've done. If you'd got any more out of him it would've been just a lot of lies. He's been laying it on good and thick with everybody he meets.'

Quinn counted out five one-pound notes. He said, 'It's only fair to give you the same as I'd have given him. What would you charge to take me on a conducted tour of the factory?'

Platt folded the money very carefully and tucked it in an inside pocket. Then he grinned for the first time.

He said, 'More than you'd earn in a month. After Wednesday's carry-on, if the works manager got to hear I'd let a stranger wander around he'd have my guts for garters.'

'Who's going to tell him?'

'Nothing doing. I'm not—' Platt stepped away from the gate and shook his head—'I'm not Reg Tugwell. He might not value his job but I need mine. I can't afford to live a gentleman's life on the strength of compensation. So . . . good day to you, mister.'

He turned and walked flat-footed to the door of the Security Office. As he brought out a key with a metal tab he looked back over his shoulder and called out, 'If you want my advice you won't loiter out there any longer. The police are kind of sensitive about this place and they might not give you a chance to explain what you were doing here.'

Then he went inside and the door swung shut. As Quinn walked back to the car he had that stray thought again— the elusive notion that had neither form nor substance.

For a while he sat looking down Centre Way with its rows of tall silent buildings on either side and the gap where new foundations were partly completed. The side road was banked with piles of earth and clay and rubble overhanging a long trench . . . duckboards half-sunk in the mire . . . a cluster of shovels . . . a motor-driven pump with a hose that had spewed out muddy water.

There was a picture in his mind of this place on a wet dark night when two people had fled with a fortune in stolen money. They had planned well and everything would have gone well—if the patrolman had not put in an appearance at the wrong time.

Violence had been no part of the scheme. It had just happened. But violence bred violence. It was almost like an unwritten law.

Quinn wondered if that night had indeed ended with an act of betrayal, if Yvonne Marshall had proved to be a cheat as well as a thief. And as he thought about her he felt a sudden chill.

. . . If I were superstitious I could describe that feeling. They say it means someone's walking over your grave . . .

More likely indigestion. That reminded him of Mrs Buchanan's warning.

'*See ye're hame sharp. Ah'll no hae ye wasting a guid meal.*'

She would walk all over him if he were late. Any dawdling and there would be no time for a quick pint on his way home. He needed a drink. It might get rid of that creepy-crawly feeling.

Dr Young would say it was post-influenzal depression. Maybe it was. On the other hand, maybe what superstitious people said was nearer the truth.

CHAPTER X

AFTER HIS SUNDAY DINNER he took a short walk to shake down Mrs Buchanan's roast beef, Yorkshire pudding and a mountain of potatoes. Then he went back to the office.

Ideas for a feature article on the Jauncey payroll theft came only with difficulty. Time after time he drafted an opening paragraph, re-read it irritably and threw it in the wastepaper basket. He knew what he wanted to say but it looked no good on paper.

At the end of half an hour he had the skeleton of an article and a dozen rough notes with which to put some flesh on bare bones. But he was still dissatisfied with the result of his work. It lacked impact. Two days in bed seemed to have blunted the ability he had come to take for granted.

Eventually he went upstairs and had a strong cup of tea and borrowed a cigarette. When he came back he phoned Scotland Yard.

Hennant had gone home. Sergeant Freeson said the superintendent was taking his grandchildren to the zoo.

Quinn said, 'Anybody else but your chief and I'd feel inclined to make a highly comical remark. However, I don't want to damage our entente cordiale. Got anything new on the Jauncey case? I could use a fresh approach for the piece I'm doing.'

'Well, there is a little problem in connection with Graham's car . . . although the superintendent doesn't want it to appear in print. He says I can tell you about it in return for the information you gave him concerning your chat with Yvonne Marshall's husband. Thinks you might come up with an ingenious solution.'

'He flatters me,' Quinn said. 'But let's hear the problem.'

Freeson told him about the spare wheel in the boot of the Hillman and what had happened when Inspector Aronson checked the flat tyre. As a footnote, the sergeant mentioned the mileage that had been done by Mrs Marshall's hired car.

'. . . You see, Mr Quinn, there's a discrepancy between what it says on the clock and the actual distance she should've travelled if she'd gone to St Katherine Dock.'

'You're seven miles short,' Quinn said.

'Yes. Personally speaking, I don't think it's as important as that business with the loose valve in Graham's spare wheel. Not much doubt it was done deliberately.'

'To fix things so that Graham's car didn't leave the factory at the same time as the Cortina. Question is—why?'

'The superintendent and I got stuck there, too. It's pretty obvious who did it—'

'Mrs Marshall,' Quinn said.

'Quite so. But there doesn't seem to be any motive.'

'Yet she must've had one. It's beginning to look more and more like her husband suggested. She pulled a fast one on Graham . . . and to do it she had to immobilize his car temporarily.'

Sergeant Freeson said, 'We got as far as that. Then we ran out of steam.'

'All right, I'll think about it.'

'Very good, sir. But you won't mention this to anyone, will you?'

'Not a word,' Quinn said. 'Thank the superintendent for giving me his confidence. I may not be able to solve his problem but he's helped me to solve one of mine . . .'

He handed in his copy at four o'clock in time to catch the first edition. '. . . I deserve a medal for conduct above and beyond the call of duty. This is supposed to be my day off.'

'You were off Thursday night and all Friday.'

'Only because I was took mortal ill. The miracle is how a man newly risen from a bed of sickness could create a work of genius such as you now hold in your uncouth hand—'

'You still need a haircut,' the news editor said. 'I can recommend a barber who'll give you an estimate. He's got a motor mower.'

'Very droll.'

'Not at all. The way you look you could become a pop star . . . if only you were tone deaf. Now go and take a walk. And don't come in again until somebody's harvested your shredded wheat.'

Quinn said, 'I'll sleep on it . . . as the gardener said to her ladyship.'

His Column on Crime in Monday's *Morning Post* dealt solely with the Jauncey payroll theft. He described Harold Graham and Mrs Yvonne Marshall in detail and outlined their personal history over the past twenty years.

Identikit pictures of the missing couple headed the feature article. Quinn re-read the whole story twice on his way to Fleet Street.

. . . A widespread search is being made to trace these two people who have not been seen since the night of the robbery. Scotland Yard is anxious to interview either Graham or Mrs Marshall who may be able to help the police in their inquiries. Campbell, Simpkin and Company, loss-adjusters, acting for the insurance company, have offered a reward of £5000 for information leading to the apprehension of the thieves and to the recovery of the property pro rata.

The total amount missing from the factory safe was nearly £54,000.

With his eyes shut and the open newspaper on his lap,

Quinn sat listening to the clickety-click of the train, the hollow whine of the motors, while he thought of the story he would have liked to write. Everybody knew who had robbed the Jauncey Engineering Company . . . but it still had to be proved in law.

No warrant had yet been issued for the arrest of Mrs Marshall. She was only wanted for questioning. But the answers to those questions would almost certainly solve the mystery of what had happened at Jauncey Engineering on the night of November 4.

. . . The two of them, either singly or together, will have established themselves some place where their identity is unlikely to be suspected. If they've separated it'll make tracing them that much more difficult . . .

Yvonne Marshall could be the negative woman in the house next door or the flat on the floor above. She was bound to have changed her name, perhaps altered the colour of her hair: she might be wearing glasses, more make-up or less—but her height and her features and the colour of her eyes would be unchanged.

. . . She's the neighbour who moved in some weeks or even months ago and was then away a lot and only appeared at intervals. Now she's there all the time. Some local tradesman's delivering her groceries regularly, some milkman's leaving a pinta on her doorstep every day or every other day . . .

The discreet person who kept herself to herself would seldom go out. Her neighbours would never have cause to complain that her radio or TV were too loud. She was that quiet woman who was rarely seen.

Someone living nearby could tell the police what they wanted to know. Someone living nearby could lead them to the woman for whom they were searching.

. . . Yes, I'm pretty sure somebody's in a position to earn themselves that five thousand quid. Somebody—without realizing it—knows the whereabouts of Mrs Yvonne Marshall—the quiet woman.

He was leaving the station when he remembered that he

had not yet had a haircut. So he called in at a barber saloon in the Strand and it was almost half-past ten when he got to the office.

The phone rang before he had time to take off his raincoat. The switchboard operator said, 'Ah, there you are, Mr Quinn.'

'Very perspicacious of you,' Quinn said. 'All I have to do is answer the telephone and you know instantly where I am. Can you read tea-cups as well?'

She said stiffly, 'You know what I meant. I've tried to get you several times this morning and you weren't in. Someone was saying you'd been off with flu.'

'I was. But they snatched me from the jaws of death. And to prove it, I'm here.'

'Too bad, Mr Quinn. Still, let's hope we have better luck next time. Now would you care to listen to the message I have for you?'

Quinn said, 'Must be one of those mornings. Thought it was only me who got them. What's the message?'

'A woman phoned at a quarter to ten and wanted to speak to you. I told her you wouldn't be in until about ten o'clock and she said she'd phone again. She did . . . at twenty past ten. Sounded quite upset when you weren't there.'

'Didn't she give you any idea what she wanted?'

'No. She'd only speak to you. Got no phone at home and has to find a call-box that isn't out of order. The way she went on you'd have thought it was my fault there was vandalism.'

'I know it isn't your fault,' Quinn said. 'If she rings again I'll tell her you're the soul of rectitude.'

'Don't bother. Just stay in Editorial so that you'll be available.'

'Did she say when that'll be?'

'Some time before eleven.'

'Don't suppose you got her name?'

The girl on the switchboard said, 'She wouldn't give it. I got the impression she didn't need to because you'd know who she was and what she was upset about.'

'I wouldn't know,' Quinn said. 'But then there are so many women in my life I lose count. However, if it's what you think it is, I promise you I'll do right by our Nell.'

The call came through at ten minutes to eleven. In a timid voice, she asked, 'Are you Mr Quinn—the one who wrote that article about a robbery at some engineering works?'

'That's me. You're the lady who's phoned several times this morning, aren't you?'

'Yes. I had to speak to you . . . although it might turn out to be nothing at all. If I'm wrong I hope you won't mind . . .'

'Not in the least. Go ahead.'

'Well, it's like this . . .'

She hesitated. Quinn could hear a background rumble of traffic muted by distance.

He said, 'Perhaps you'd better tell me first who you are.'

'Oh, yes, of course. I thought—' her voice was almost lost in the traffic noises—'I thought you'd want to know that.'

There was another pause. Then she asked, 'Does anyone get the reward if they tell the police where that woman Marshall is living?'

Quinn suppressed his immediate reaction. This was only the forerunner of many calls from people who would be sure they knew what the authorities wanted to know. His column was bound to have that effect if it served any purpose at all.

Every policeman had experience of the cranks and neurotics who came forward when a crime attained wide publicity. This woman might well be one of the type who even confessed to murder in their desire to attract attention.

While the thought still lingered in his mind, she said, 'You see, before I'm prepared to say any more, I've got to be sure I'll get the money you say they've offered for information.'

'Depends how much of the stolen money they recover,' Quinn said. 'You get a proportionate amount of the reward.'

'I've only—' a touch of obstinacy came into her voice— 'I've only your word for that.'

'If you don't believe me why did you bother phoning? Incidentally, you should've informed the police instead of—'

'No, that's what I won't do. They'll tie me up in all sorts of red tape and at the finish I'll get nothing. You know how to handle officials and so I felt I'd be better talking to you. As I say, it was your article that made me put two and two together . . . although I could be wrong.'

'Only way to find out is to tell me what you know—or think you know,' Quinn said.

The phone made a hissing noise like the sound of steam escaping from an old-fashioned railway engine. Then she said, 'All right, I will. I'm Mrs Wentworth and I live at Hilary Close. It's a block of flats in Longford Road.'

'Where is that?'

'Earl's Court. The woman I'm talking about is in No. 11. My flat is No. 10, the one next door.'

'What name does she go under?'

'She calls herself Mrs Cooke.'

'How long has she lived there?'

'Well, she took No. 11 about three or four months ago but, until last week, she was only here for a few days at a time. Then I might not see her for a week or two. She was more often away from the flat than in it.'

'Is this Mrs Cooke there, now?'

'Yes.'

'When did she return?'

'Last Wednesday night. I didn't see her but there was a light on in her kitchen when I came home from my mother's. That would be about nine o'clock. I noticed it particularly because the place had been in darkness for at least ten days before then.'

Once again the phone hissed and puffed. Quinn said, 'You're sure it was Wednesday night?'

'Positive. I only go to my mother's on a Wednesday and a Sunday . . . and I know it wasn't yesterday when I first saw Mrs Cooke's light on and heard somebody moving about. Like I told you, her flat is next to mine and I can hear—'

'Yes, I understand. Have you seen her since Wednesday?'

'Twice. Last Thursday and again this morning. It was after I'd read your article . . . so I tried to get a good look at her. After all, she is the kind of stranger you described. And you never know, do you?'

Quinn said, 'No, you're right. Is she alone or is there a man in the flat?'

'Not this time. But when she was here before I have seen a man coming and going. That would be about a month ago.'

'Did he answer the description in the *Morning Post*?'

'Well, he was the right height and build . . . from what I remember of him.'

'Not much to go by,' Quinn said. 'Does the woman resemble Mrs Marshall?'

'Except for the colour of her hair. It's blonde—the kind that could hardly be natural. Got grey eyes and a slim figure and I'd say she's about thirty. Very good-looking. Something nice about her, as well. I can hardly believe she's the kind of young woman who'd do a thing like that. Perhaps I'm making a mistake. If I am—'

'There'll be no harm done,' Quinn said. 'Has she ever spoken to you?'

'No. The most she's ever done is smile as she's gone past on the stairs. Only happened half a dozen times . . . if that.'

'What about the man you used to see? Ever hear him speak?'

'Not once. Never even wished me the time of day. Always looked in the other direction. Of course, that might not mean anything.'

'As you say. Nevertheless, I'd like to take a look at the woman in Flat 11. Where are you calling from, Mrs Wentworth?'

'A phone box in Longford Road. When will you be coming here?'

'I'm on my way right now. Please go straight home and wait for me. If you should see this woman who calls herself Mrs Cooke don't show any interest in her.'

'Do you think she really is Mrs Marshall?'

'I'm willing to bet on it,' Quinn said. 'So don't scare her away. If you do, it could cost you five thousand pounds.'

Hilary Close formed three sides of a rectangle enclosing well-kept lawns bisected by a tarmac roadway from which flagged paths radiated to the various entrances. Flats 10 and 11 were in the left-hand block.

As he climbed the stairs, Quinn had a feeling that he was hoping for too much. Thousands of people must have read his Column on Crime that Monday morning. Many of them would be persuading themselves that the couple next door were Harold Graham and Yvonne Marshall, wanted for the Jauncey payroll theft.

Mrs Wentworth might merely be grafting a newspaper description on to some perfectly innocent neighbours. To her they looked like the missing couple because that was how she wanted them to look. It could be nothing more than a form of wish-fulfilment.

Soon he would know. Either it was all a waste of time ... or Mrs Wentworth would have found her pot of gold at the foot of the rainbow.

He heard a car drive away from somewhere behind the centre block and the thought came to him that he might be too late. Beyond that thought lurked another which his mind tried to reject.

If the woman in Flat 11 was Yvonne Marshall ... and Graham was hiding behind a door as he had hidden on the night of the robbery ... and this time he might strike too hard ...

When Quinn reached the second floor, he was ready to turn back. This kind of thing should be tackled by the police. No one had paid him to risk his neck ... or get his head bashed in.

Then he was outside the door of Flat 10. As he reached out to press the bell-push he told himself he had passed the point of no return.

CHAPTER XI

Mrs Wentworth had skimpy black hair, an elfin face and round black eyes with the watchful expression of a bird. She looked both excited and afraid at the same time.

In a voice little more than a whisper, she asked, 'Mr Quinn?'

'Yes.'

One hand pushed the door open wider, the other hand beckoned him to come inside. There was just enough room to squeeze past her.

They went into the kitchen, where soiled dishes from breakfast still lay on the table. Several pans were piled in the sink. A bread-board littered with crumbs stood on the working-surface.

She studied Quinn intently from head to foot, her mouth compressed in a small tight ring. Then she said very softly, 'I'd take you into the sitting-room but Mrs Cooke might hear us talking through the wall. You see, her room is next to ours. So I hope you don't mind me bringing you in here.'

Quinn said, 'I don't mind at all. When you saw your neighbour this morning was she going out or coming in?'

'She was just taking in the milk. I only got a glimpse of her.'

'Did you hear her moving around before you went out to phone?'

'Yes. You can't tell what they're doing but the wall's not very thick and you know somebody's there.'

'You rang the *Morning Post* twice before you eventually got me at ten minutes to eleven,' Quinn said. 'Did you come back here each time?'

'Oh, yes. The phone box I used is only two minutes' walk away. It's more often than not out of order but it was working today. You'd never believe the trouble we've had with young vandals. My husband says the only way to stop it is to make an example of the next bunch of hooligans they catch . . .'

She had a wet mouth and she kept giving Quinn little sidelong glances that made him feel uncomfortable. He vaguely wondered if her phone call had been nothing but a pretext to get a man into the flat while she was alone.

It was an absurd idea . . . quite absurd. Yet such things were not altogether unknown. The quicker he got away the better. No sense in asking for trouble.

He said, 'Was Mrs Cooke in her flat just before you went out to phone me at ten to eleven?'

'Definitely. Her radio was on. I could hear some music programme.'

'Was it still on when you came back?'

'Not the music. It was one of those talks for schools.'

'The walls certainly can't be very thick,' Quinn said. 'But I didn't hear any radio in Flat 11 when I came upstairs. Would you like to go into the sitting-room and see if it's on now?'

Mrs Wentworth gave him another sidelong glance. For a moment she stood moistening her lips. Then she went out and left him alone in the kitchen.

He heard a door open . . . footsteps crossing a carpeted floor. And after that there was no sound except the rumble of traffic down below in Longford Road.

His ideas about Mrs Wentworth urged him to think of some excuse to leave. He could find an opportunity later to check up on Flat 11 without involving this woman with the predatory mouth.

While he was rehearsing the right thing to say, she came back into the kitchen. She said, 'Yes, the radio's still on. But she's turned the volume down. I can barely hear it. Makes me wonder if she's listening to us?'

Quinn told himself it was possible. Even if it were, it was no proof that the woman who called herself Mrs Cooke was in fact Mrs Yvonne Marshall. It might mean only that Mrs Wentworth's neighbour was as curious about her as she was about Mrs Cooke.

Yet ... Now was the time to settle the matter beyond doubt. Later might be too late. If it was Mrs Marshall and he let her escape ...

He asked, 'Could you find some pretext for calling on her?'

Once again Mrs Wentworth made her mouth into a little moist button. Then she said, 'I wouldn't know what to say. We've never exchanged two words since she came here.'

'Suppose you told her you'd been expecting a visitor—your mother, for instance? You wondered if she'd called while you were out just before eleven o'clock, if Mrs Cooke had heard her ringing your bell. It's the kind of thing you might do, isn't it?'

'Yes ... yes, I might ... if we'd spoken to each other before. But we haven't.'

'Then you're making this an excuse to get on speaking terms. Can't do any harm to let her think so.'

For a long time Mrs Wentworth stood thinking, her round black eyes fixed on Quinn's face. At last, she said, 'All right. But I don't see what good it will do.'

'It'll give me the chance to get a look at her.'

'How?'

'I'll come out on to the landing while she's talking to you,' Quinn said.

'But she'll see you there. Don't you mind?'

'No. I've nothing to be afraid of. She's the one who doesn't want to be seen ... if she really is Yvonne Marshall.'

Mrs Wentworth took another ten seconds to make up her mind. Then she said, 'You're quite right. I'll do it.'

He followed her out of the flat and watched her hesitate before she reached for the bell-push of No. 11. He saw her stop before she touched it. With her hand poised she went very still.

Quinn asked, 'What's wrong?'

She stepped back and looked at him over her shoulder. She said, 'The door's open. It hasn't been shut properly. If I ring the bell I'll push it open more.'

'That won't be your fault,' Quinn said. 'You won't be trespassing. Go ahead and ring it.'

The sound of the bell lasted only a moment. The door scarcely moved under the pressure of Mrs Wentworth's finger. When she took her hand away she looked at Quinn again.

There was no sound inside Flat 11 except the faint music of a radio. He could hear it now. He would probably have heard it when he was coming up the stairs if he had specially listened.

Mrs Wentworth was still looking at him. He wondered if she needed him to tell her why nothing stirred in Flat 11. It was so obvious . . . so very obvious. All her coming and going, those three trips to the phone box, had aroused the suspicions of the woman who called herself Mrs Cooke.

When she left her hired car at the Neptune Garage she had used the name Whitelaw. But names meant nothing. She was the same woman.

Now she had gone. He had missed the chance of a lifetime. And the galling feature was that it had been his own fault. That lost half-hour had made all the difference.

. . . If I hadn't stopped to get a haircut before I went to the office I'd have been there the first time Mrs Wentworth phoned. So I'd have got here that much earlier. And Yvonne Marshall, alias Mrs Cooke, would've had no reason to suspect that her secret was known . . .

He brushed past Mrs Wentworth and drummed his knuckles on the door of Flat 11. It swung open another inch or two. He pushed it back against the wall.

Then he took a step inside and called out, 'Mrs Cooke? Are you there, Mrs Cooke?'

It was a useless charade. He knew she had fled. If this eventuality had been foreseen she must have prepared a second escape-route. The military called it defence in depth.

No panic. As soon as she guessed that a neighbour was showing undue interest in her she prepared to move out. Even if she were wrong it was better than being caught in a trap of her own making.

With money in abundance she could have established two hide-outs. Now Mrs Cooke had become Mrs X . . . with a different-coloured wig in a different style. And he had robbed himself of a damn good story.

In a tart voice, Mrs Wentworth said, 'There's no one in the flat. She must've left the radio playing so I'd think she was still here. Heaven knows where she is by this time.'

'At least, she's on the run,' Quinn said. 'Should make it easier for the police to find her.'

'That's not much satisfaction to me. I won't get a penny of the reward. If I'd gone to the police straight away this would never have happened.'

'Well, no one stopped you. I suggested it myself but you didn't want to have any dealings with the police and—'

'It would've been too late by then. By wasting time over you I've let five thousand pounds slip through my fingers.'

Quinn said, 'What you've never had you never miss . . . so they say. Let's take a look around and see if there's anything we can salvage.'

With a sulky look, Mrs Wentworth asked, 'What if she isn't Mrs Marshall, after all? What if she comes back and finds you snooping around?'

'I'll take that risk. You can wait outside if you like.'

She hesitated on the doorstep for a moment when he went in. Then she followed him.

Three doors led off the little narrow hall. One was a broom cupboard. It faced a bedroom overlooking Longford Road.

There were twin beds, two wardrobes, two bedside tables, individual reading-lamps above each bed, a dressing-table on which stood a collection of cosmetics in bottles and jars and fancy containers. The fitted nylon bedspreads with a deep flounce reaching almost to the floor matched the dull gold of the carpet.

A pair of fluffy mules lay beside the nearer bed on which a sheer nightdress had been laid across the mounded pillow. The radio they had heard was an expensive portable standing on the bedside table. He switched it off.

Everything in the room looked new. Carpet, curtains and furniture had seen very little use. The whole place reminded Quinn of a display in one of the West End stores.

He opened the wardrobe next to the window. It was empty.

The other wardrobe contained a dress, a trouser-suit and a coat with a fur collar. A pair of shoes rested on the double rail down at floor level.

There were stockings and underwear and various items of clothing in the dressing-table drawers. Nothing seemed to have been disturbed.

Quinn told himself Yvonne Marshall could afford the sacrifice of her few possessions. Including the furniture and anything else there might be in the flat the whole lot could be replaced for a couple of thousand. That would be cheap compared with her liberty.

Close behind him, Mrs Wentworth said, 'Didn't take very much with her, did she? Looks as if she just got up and left.'

'With fifty-four thousand pounds she won't go short of a dress to wear or a bed to sleep in,' Quinn said.

The sitting-room was comfortably furnished. All the bits and pieces in here also were new. He had no doubt the same applied to the rest of the flat.

Kitchen . . . bathroom . . . toilet . . . So far he had found nothing to indicate the personality of Mrs Yvonne Marshall, nothing to betray where she had gone.

Only one room remained. He knew it would tell him no more than all the others.

Mrs Wentworth said, 'That'll be the second bedroom. All these flats are much the same. We use ours as a snug where we watch TV.'

She opened the door and glanced in and added, 'Couple of suitcases . . . that's all.'

Quinn listened with only half his mind. He was thinking that Yvonne Marshall had probably kept an overnight bag ready packed with things she would need if she had to leave in a hurry.

. . . Might even happen that she would have to put up at a hotel because she couldn't get to her next destination . . . wherever that is. I don't know why but it's possible

she might not want to go straight there. Taken all round it isn't the only thing I don't know . . .

Further back in his mind he had a picture of an empty wardrobe that should have contained a man's clothes. But there was nothing anywhere belonging to a man.

Twin beds, each with its own reading-lamp . . . two wardrobes . . . a bathroom cabinet with one half unused . . . no razor or shaving soap or blades . . . only one tube of toothpaste and one brush . . . only one towel on the heated rail.

Something was wrong: two beds and only one used: two wardrobes and only one used: half the shelves in the bathroom cabinet empty: one toothbrush . . .

Picture after picture revolved in his mind like a television set with a faulty horizontal hold. Then it locked on the image of a single toothbrush.

If Mrs Marshall had kept an overnight bag for use in just this type of emergency it was bound to include a toothbrush. Yvonne Marshall would have seen to that . . . like she had seen to everything else.

Graham had thought his plan was perfect. But he had been hoodwinked by someone who had outmanoeuvred him on the last lap.

Quinn's thoughts shifted to what the police would say. He had to tell them how Yvonne Marshall had escaped . . . and why she had got away . . . and whose fault it was . . .

That was when Mrs Wentworth took another couple of steps into the second bedroom. Quinn saw her pick up one of the suitcases and turn to face him.

Then her round black eyes seemed to shrink in her head and she made a noise as though she were about to be sick. Her hand let go of the suitcase. On stiff legs she went back, step by step, until she bumped against the opposite wall.

All the time she was trying to speak. And at last she said in a hoarse dry voice that was barely audible '. . . My God . . . oh, my God . . .'

From where Quinn stood he could see almost the whole of the twelve-by-fourteen room. Only the area behind the door was hidden from him. That was where Mrs Wentworth's terrified eyes were fixed.

Afterwards he had no recollection of going inside, no recollection of skirting the open door until he was able to see the hidden corner of the room. Afterwards he remembered only what he saw lying close to the wall.

She lay face down, her arms outstretched, her head towards the door, her fingers like claws digging into the carpet. One shoe had come off. The back of her dress was ripped apart almost to the waist. Something that looked like a nylon stocking had been knotted tightly round her neck.

There were other things that Quinn saw: bruises on her bare arms, a disordered blonde wig revealing brown hair underneath, a clip-on ear-ring on the carpet, blood that had welled from a gash in the lobe of her ear.

They told him she had struggled for her life, that she had continued fighting even while someone squatted on her back and drew the stocking tighter and tighter until all her frantic strength had gone. Broken fingernails testified to the frenzy of that hopeless struggle.

He took hold of her wrist and found it was as warm as though she were still alive. But there was no pulse. She might not have been dead very long but her skin had the feel of death.

Mrs Wentworth came away from the wall. She was breathing noisily like a woman who had run to the limit of her endurance.

In a ragged voice, she said, 'That's her . . . that's Mrs Cooke. It's the same dress I saw when she was bringing in the milk. She's dead . . . isn't she?'

Quinn said, 'Not much doubt about it. I'd guess she was strangled while you were speaking to me on the phone at ten minutes to eleven.'

'You mean someone visited her when I was out?'

'Probably. Whoever it was must've turned the radio down before slipping out so that it wouldn't sound too loud when the door was opened.'

Mrs Wentworth was breathing more slowly now. She crossed the room in a series of little hesitant steps until she reached the doorway.

Then she asked, 'Do you think it was that man she ran away with?'

'Could be.'

'Why would he want to kill her? I thought they were supposed to be lovers.'

'What's supposed and what is are often two different things,' Quinn said.

'But if it wasn't him who else could it have been?'

'I don't know. And I'm not even prepared to make a guess. It isn't my job.'

With a look of morbid fascination, Mrs Wentworth asked, 'Aren't you going to call the police?'

Quinn said, 'No, you are. I'll stay here and see nothing's disturbed. Go and find a telephone—not the one in this flat—and tell them the woman in No. 11 has been attacked and you think she's dead. Know how to dial 999?'

'Yes, of course.'

'Good. If any of your neighbours are on the phone it'll save time.'

Mrs Wentworth sidled out of the room as though afraid of turning her back. When she was safely in the hall, she said, 'I'll ask the old man downstairs. He's usually in about now . . .'

Quinn walked from sitting-room to main bedroom and back to sitting-room, time after time, while he waited. He had no wish to maintain a death-watch beside the woman who had died with a twisted stocking knotted round her neck.

Whatever her sins she had paid in full. Death had come the hard way. This could only be the work of someone obsessed by hatred.

Money—even as much as fifty-four thousand pounds—would not have been sufficient motive. For money alone there had been no need to kill . . . and kill with brutal violence.

Yet the money had gone. He found a handbag in the sitting-room but all it contained was the usual stuff a woman carried—that and thirty-odd pounds in notes and silver:

no car keys, no driving licence, no means of identification.

Yvonne Marshall had evidently planned to use hired transport when the time came for her to travel on. The removal van that took her furniture would also have taken Jauncey Engineering's payroll, secure in a locked blanket chest or two or three suitcases or a stout wooden box labelled: *Crockery—Fragile.*

So many ways from which to choose . . . At that Quinn remembered there were a couple of travelling cases in the room where her body lay.

He was reluctant to go near her again but he had to satisfy his curiosity. Without looking behind the open door he went in and picked up the two cases.

They were empty. He could tell that by their weight alone. If they had ever contained the payroll money, if she had transferred it from the small attaché cases, it was gone now.

It weighed roughly eighty pounds. That meant forty pounds in each hand if carried in two bags. A man could hardly go far loaded like a slave Negro.

And it would have to be done in one trip. He dared not risk coming back. So it must all have been in two travelling cases similar to those in the spare room where Yvonne Marshall had met her death.

Unless the money was hidden somewhere else . . . unless it had never been brought to the flat in Hilary Close. The cases could have been intended for some other purpose.

There Quinn wondered how she came to be murdered in that little unfurnished room. He was still wondering when two uniformed policemen arrived in a patrol car.

They were followed within minutes by a police doctor . . . and then the local chief inspector . . . and fingerprint men . . . and a photographer. Not long afterwards, Detective-Superintendent Hennant arrived, accompanied by Sergeant Freeson.

CHAPTER XII

PIPER HEARD THE NEWS just as he was about to go home. He said, 'I wouldn't take Hennant's comments too much to heart if I were you. After all, you did advise this Mrs Wentworth to get in touch with the police. You're not responsible because she didn't.'

'The superintendent's attitude is that I should've done it myself,' Quinn said.

'That's a matter of opinion. She didn't tell you she had proof: only that she suspected the identity of the woman next door. It might've been no more than something she imagined after reading your article in the *Morning Post*.'

'So I kept telling him.'

'You could also have told him Mrs Wentworth wouldn't have suspected anything if it had not been for that very good piece of yours. I had a feeling it would produce results . . . if anything could.'

Quinn said, 'Praise from you is praise indeed. Glad I phoned you. It's boosted my morale.'

'Nonsense. Nothing wrong with your morale. You rang me for some other reason. So, come on. Out with it.'

'Well, to be honest—'

'That's often a cover-up for deception,' Piper said.

'—something about the flat in Earl's Court has been niggling at me. I thought, with all due respect—'

'And that usually precedes a rude remark,' Piper said.

'No, I mean it. I was going to say I thought of trying it on the dog . . . in other words, you.'

'Trying what?'

'This thing I keep remembering. The more I think about it the less sense it makes. I didn't mention it to Superintendent Hennant because I wanted to get away before he threw me out.'

'So you'd like me to do some thinking about it?'

'Yes . . . if you don't mind.'

'Oh, I don't mind at all. I'll be glad to help if I can . . . providing it's not a lengthy problem. I promised I'd take Jane to the theatre tonight.'

Quinn felt the old barrier come down between them. It was foolish of him—foolish to the point of childishness—but he had no way of overcoming it.

This had never happened before Piper remarried. There had been times when they might not have seen each other for months but the easy familiarity of their relationship had remained unimpaired.

Until Jane came along . . . After that, Quinn was odd-man-out. Rightly or wrongly, that was how he had felt ever since. To deny it did no good.

He said, 'I'm sorry. I didn't know you were in a hurry. Let's leave it for the time being and—'

'Not at all. I didn't say I was in a desperate hurry. Five minutes is neither here nor there.'

'If you're sure . . .'

'Quite sure. So go ahead. The dog's listening.'

'OK. This is tied up with that business of the flat tyres on Graham's car. Not much doubt it happened at Jauncey's factory and even less doubt that Yvonne Marshall was the one who unscrewed the valve so that he wouldn't get away at the same time as she did. Are you with me?'

Piper said, 'No. I don't know what you're talking about. This is the first time I've heard that Mrs Marshall let down one of Graham's tyres. There was no mention of it in the papers.'

'I'd forgotten that,' Quinn said. 'Well, the thing actually came to light when a police inspector examined the boot of Graham's car. He noticed that the spare wheel was muddy and the mud hadn't had time to dry. For at least a week prior to last Wednesday night there had been no rain and so . . .'

He repeated the story he had heard from Sergeant Freeson about a sneak-thief called Mick Pavitt. It took only a couple of minutes.

Then Quinn went on, '. . . She got well away while

Graham was changing his spare wheel. He wouldn't suspect she'd done it. Simple but effective, eh?'

'Yes, but where's your problem—the thing you say is niggling you? What was there in the flat that you keep remembering?'

'Two beds, two bedside tables, two bedside lamps, two wardrobes,' Quinn said.

After he had thought about it, Piper asked, 'Anything to indicate the kind of person who's been living there with her?'

'No, not a thing anywhere. The flat was furnished for two but only occupied by one.'

'And you think she hadn't intended to live there on her own?'

'Stands to reason. Otherwise, why two of everything?'

'Many bedrooms have a pair of wardrobes,' Piper said.

'I wouldn't doubt it. Lots of widows have also got twin beds. But Mrs Marshall wasn't a widow continuing to use furniture she'd bought before she became a widow. All this stuff was newly bought and newly installed: both beds, both bedside tables, both lamps. I've added it up a score of times and I always get the wrong answer.'

'Have you got an idea there's another man involved?'

Quinn said, 'That didn't take the mind of a genius. But it can't be the right answer.'

'Why not?'

'Because, if it is, we've got more questions than we had before. First of all, who is he?'

'Let's skip that and take your second question,' Piper said.

'OK. Why no sign that he'd ever been in the place—not a single thing to show she hadn't lived there alone since she took refuge in the flat on Wednesday night?'

'Perhaps he wasn't due to arrive until later.'

'All right—perhaps. But what would've happened when he did? Mrs Wentworth had seen Yvonne Marshall's supposed husband a few times. Admittedly she couldn't describe him but she'd have been bound to spot that husband No. 2 wasn't anything like husband No. 1.'

Piper said, 'Suggestion withdrawn. They wouldn't want to stir up any gossip.'

'Of course not. Now you're beginning to understand why I've had a little mouse running around inside my head ever since I looked into that bedroom. Taken by and large it's a queer business, isn't it?'

'More than queer. It's also contagious.'

'What does that mean?'

'There's a question you haven't asked,' Piper said. 'If the man whom Mrs Wentworth saw a few weeks ago wasn't Harold Graham but some other man establishing an identity as Mrs Cooke's husband . . . then how did Graham catch up with the woman who called herself Mrs Cooke?'

Quinn said, 'I hate to steal any credit from you but I thought of that five minutes after I saw her lying dead on the floor. Incidentally, the police surgeon says she'd received a blow on the head shortly before death took place. He's of the opinion it would've knocked her half-unconscious . . . but that's subject to the findings of the post-mortem.'

'If she put up a struggle she must've been only dazed.'

'Yes, I suppose so. Don't imagine we'll ever know for sure exactly what did happen.'

Piper looked at his watch. There was still time.

He said, 'This may strike you as an absurd question . . . but has anyone identified the dead woman?'

'Not all that absurd,' Quinn said. 'A better word is perceptive. But you can stop thinking along those lines. A bloke called Keith Marshall was sent for and he says definitely that the woman known as Mrs Cooke was his wife. Now I'll leave you to meditate on the problem of the twin beds.'

'No, don't ring off yet. If Graham didn't know where Mrs Marshall was living, it couldn't have been Graham who killed her. Evidently someone else is involved.'

'Yes, but who? Up to now everything has pointed to the fact that she double-crossed Graham and left him flat on his whatsit.'

'Maybe so. If she did, her only hope of getting away with

it was to make sure he didn't find out where she'd gone the night of the robbery.'

'Which brings us back to the man Mrs Wentworth saw coming and going,' Quinn said.

'Can you think of an alternative?'

'Not at the moment. But if Yvonne Marshall had another man he could've been the one who strangled her. The question is—why?'

There seemed only one answer. It was a case of the biter bit. And yet . . . Piper told himself that too many people had already jumped to hasty conclusions.

He said, 'We might consider the possibility that he didn't need her any more. She had the stolen money . . . and she'd shaken off Graham. With him out of the way, she was the only thing that stood between the second man and fifty thousands pounds all for himself.'

'It's not a bad theory,' Quinn said. 'If you're right, the money must've been in Yvonne's possession.'

'That's fairly obvious.'

'Yes . . . but he'd have had to lug a heavy load from the flat to wherever he'd parked his vehicle without being seen. Assuming the notes were packed in two separate bags, each one would've been a good forty pounds dead weight. That's quite something to cart around.'

Piper asked, 'Did you see a car or van outside when you got there?'

'No.'

'Then we can take it he'd already gone.'

'I might've just missed him,' Quinn said. 'I heard the sound of an engine somewhere behind the centre block of flats as I arrived. Of course, it could've been somebody else. And another thing . . .'

'Yes?'

'There were two empty suitcases in Flat 11. What did he use to carry the money in?'

'Two other cases, I should imagine. Nobody knows how many pieces of luggage she had.'

Quinn said, 'That's a point. I've got myself so tied up

with ifs and buts I can't see for looking. All the same . . .'

'What now?'

'I still say that a bag weighing forty pounds in each hand would take a bit of carrying.'

'That could explain why you found the outside door open.'

'Meaning he had both hands occupied?'

'Yes. Of course, he could've put one bag down—'

'But he was in too big a hurry. So he must've tried to pull the door shut with his foot.'

'And it didn't latch properly,' Piper said.

Time was getting short. If he talked any longer on the phone he would be late.

This thing was less straightforward than it looked. A glib explanation solved nothing. From the very beginning, too many people had adjusted the known circumstances to fit their own preconceived ideas. And where there were gaps they had made unwarranted assumptions.

Quinn asked, 'Are you convinced that's what happened?'

It would do no good to pretend. Piper said, 'Far from it. I need to re-think the whole affair. Come and see me in the morning . . .'

At a quarter past six, Quinn made another phone call. Superintendent Hennant was at a conference in the Assistant Commissioner's room but Sergeant Freeson was available.

He said, 'No, I'd say you're forgiven by now. Just mind your step. This case is getting the superintendent kind of rattled. Robbery is one thing but murder's a different kettle of fish.'

'I'm not to blame because somebody tied a nylon stocking round Yvonne Marshall's neck.'

'Blame isn't exactly the word I'd use but, all the same, it's possible that you inspired what took place this morning . . . innocently, of course.'

Quinn had a bout of coughing. When he got over it, he

asked, 'Innocently or otherwise, how could I have inspired any such thing?'

'With that article of yours in the *Morning Post*. Our opinion is that you threw a scare into Harold Graham and he got rid of Mrs Marshall so she wouldn't fall into our hands and be persuaded to talk.'

'I was only doing my job. Furthermore, you people wanted all the publicity you could get.'

'Quite so, Mr Quinn. I don't want you to think anyone's criticizing you.'

'Thanks,' Quinn said. 'I was afraid you'd have me thrown in the Tower. And, while we're on the subject, why should Graham be afraid Yvonne might talk if you picked her up? What could she say that you didn't already know?'

'Well, for one thing, she'd have told us where the money was hidden.'

'He could've taken care of that by shifting the payroll somewhere else. There was no need to kill her.'

'We can't hope to read what went on in his mind,' Freeson said.

'Maybe not. And that brings us to the real reason for this call. I've been wondering, Sergeant, if it was Graham who strangled her.'

'I shouldn't think there was any doubt about that, Mr Quinn. For your information, we've discarded the theory that she double-crossed him.'

'Oh, you have, have you?'

'Yes. The pity is that we paid so much attention to it from the start. Merely sent us off on a wild-goose chase.'

'What about the flat tyre? Someone must've unscrewed the valve and if so—'

'Not necessarily, Mr Quinn. It could just have happened.'

'And the dust cap? Did that just happen, as well?'

'Wouldn't be the first time,' Freeson said. 'More than once, when I've had my tyres checked, the lad at the garage has left the cap off altogether.'

'So your bet is that it was Graham who visited Flat 11

this morning and tied a stocking round poor Yvonne's neck?'

'That's right, Mr Quinn. Why should we complicate the affair for no good reason?'

Quinn said, 'I can give you a good reason for one complication. If Graham knew Mrs Marshall was living at Hilary Close, why didn't he set up house there with her?'

'That's something we don't know. At the moment it isn't really important. The main thing is—'

'What makes you say it isn't important? That flat was specially chosen as a hideout. Months before the theft took place, Mrs Marshall established a new identity for herself in Earl's Court. Soon as she and Graham skipped with Jauncey's payroll she took up residence at No. 11. Why didn't he do likewise?'

'I've no idea,' Freeson said. 'When we catch him perhaps he'll tell us.'

'If is a better word than when. Wherever he's been since last Wednesday night it must be a pretty secure place. And that's where he's gone now—along with fifty-four thousand quid . . . assuming it was Harold Graham. But I doubt it, Sergeant, I doubt it very much.'

'Because you still think he didn't know where she went after she left the factory?'

Something in the sergeant's voice made Quinn feel he was being laughed at. He said, 'I've got a hunch you're taking the mick out of me. What have you found out since I had that cosy session with Superintendent Hennant?'

'Just this, Mr Quinn. Graham's known all along about the flat in Hilary Close. We can now prove it.'

'How?'

'We showed an Identikit picture of Harold Graham to Mrs Wentworth, the woman in No. 10. She says he was the man she saw on a number of occasions entering or leaving the next-door flat. His last visit, as far as she's aware, was prior to last Wednesday night when the woman who called herself Mrs Cooke returned.'

'Mrs W. is quite sure it was the same man?'

'Absolutely. She hadn't been able to describe him . . . but one look at the picture was enough. She'll swear to it any time we like.'

'So that's that,' Quinn said.

'Oh, yes. There's no question that Mrs Marshall wouldn't have gone anywhere near the flat in Hilary Close if she'd wanted to escape from Graham.'

'Which means she didn't plan to cheat him out of his share of the money.'

'In the light of events, quite the reverse. When she'd served her purpose she was expendable. Whether it was a snap decision or a long-term plan is immaterial.'

'Makes no odds to Yvonne,' Quinn said.

He could see the bloated flesh of her neck bulging out on either side of the nylon stocking, her tongue protruding from her open mouth, her hands like claws frozen in a final act of desperation. Harold Graham could have arranged a more merciful end for his accomplice . . . but he had chosen this way. It must have been a matter of choice.

That was what made her death all the more terrible. Not only had it been necessary for her to die. The method used had ensured that she died with the maximum suffering.

. . . Whatever she was guilty of she's paid twice over. He didn't need to kill her at all. If he wanted the whole fifty-odd thousand for himself he only had to take it and get out. She represented no danger to him. So what he did was cold-blooded and deliberate . . .

Sergeant Freeson was saying, '. . . must've done something pretty bad. Wonder why he hated her so much?'

A woman's voice echoed in Quinn's mind—a nice looking young woman with blonde hair and warm brown eyes. Once again he could hear her talking to him as he stood in the porch of the house in Maryland Avenue.

'*. . . I know Harold. Normally he's a good-natured man but he has a temper when he's roused.*'

'Doesn't matter now,' Quinn said. 'She's beyond hate or love or greed or any other emotion that made her tick. The only important thing is that Graham's disappeared again. And, if you want my opinion, you'll never find him.'

'Unless—' Sergeant Freeson sounded unperturbed—'unless he gets careless and makes a mistake.'

Quinn had a fleeting thought of Yvonne Marshall who had met death on the threshold of a new life. He said, 'Men like Harold Graham don't make mistakes.'

CHAPTER XIII

TUESDAY, November 10, was another grey morning with dark clouds that scurried before a blustering wind. There had been heavy rain during the night and more was forecast.

The first drops spattered the pavement as Quinn came out of Piccadilly Circus underground into Regent Street. By the time he reached the corner of Vigo Street rain was trickling off his unkempt hair. He ran the last fifty yards.

On his way upstairs he mopped his face and wiped the inside of his collar with a damp handkerchief. He felt uncomfortably wet when he knocked on Piper's door and walked in.

The little room overlooking Vigo Street was warm with the heat of a glowing gas-fire. Condensation misted the window and made a hazy picture of the narrow winding street below.

Piper had his back to the fire. On his desk lay a small heap of unopened correspondence.

He said, 'Take your coat off and come over here and dry out. How far have you walked?'

'Only from Piccadilly Circus. That's where it started chucking it down.'

'You look as if you're soaked through.'

'I feel as if I've just been fished out of the Thames,' Quinn said. 'If you wouldn't mind moving away so I can get a glimpse of the fire . . . thanks.'

His face was paler than usual and he seemed to have lost weight since the last time they had met. Piper said, 'You shouldn't be out in this weather. You haven't got over the flu yet.'

Quinn said, 'You and Mrs Buchanan must be reading from the same script. Not that I don't appreciate your solicitude . . . but I assure you I'm all right. At least, I'm as right as I'll ever be.'

'You should take more care of yourself. Why don't you find some nice girl and get married?'

'A nice girl wouldn't have me,' Quinn said.

'I'm being serious.'

'No, you're being morbid.'

'All right. I was only trying to give you some good advice. But have it your own way.'

Quinn said, 'That's what the actress said to the bishop. Now, if you don't mind, I'd like to tell you what I heard from Sergeant Freeson after I'd spoken to you yesterday . . .'

He dried himself in front of the fire while he talked about the Identikit picture Mrs Wentworth had recognized, the mileage recorded by the speedometer of a pale green Cortina and Freeson's comments on a tyre with a loose valve.

'. . . Not much doubt how Scotland Yard feel about the information I got from Mrs Marshall's husband. More or less blame me for putting them on the wrong tack. And all I did was hand them a theory based on Marshall's opinion of his wife.'

'Wouldn't have made any difference whether they were on the wrong or the right track,' Piper said. 'I felt all along that everybody had been too quick to accept that she betrayed Graham and went off with Jauncey's payroll . . . but it didn't get me anywhere. And this Identikit picture business doesn't alter my ideas.'

'Which are?'

'Well, first of all, that simple answers are almost invariably the best. A man and a woman conspired to rob their employers of a large sum of money. They succeeded. Under a false name she took up residence in a block of flats at Earl's Court—'

'With the proceeds of the robbery,' Quinn said.

'That's only an assumption—the first of several which

confuse the main issue.'

'But the cash must be somewhere.'

'Oh, yes. The question, however, is—why there?'

'Because she had it when she drove away from the factory. Reg Tugwell, the patrolman, saw half a dozen of the cases containing the money in the boot of her hired car. Since she left the Cortina at the Neptune Garage about an hour later we know she didn't swap cars with Graham. Or would you call that an assumption, too?'

Piper said, 'If it is, it's a reasonable one. The time available and the mileage registered on the clock would indicate that she called at Hilary Close. She must've had some reason for making the detour.'

'And that was to deliver something. What else but the payroll money?'

'It seems logical, I admit. Nevertheless, it poses one big question. How did she get those attaché cases into her flat?'

Quinn half-turned to toast his other side at the fire. He said, 'She carried them upstairs. It's only one flight. What other way is there?'

'None. And that's the point. The average woman would find it difficult—if not impossible—to carry more than one case in each hand. At that, the total weight would be between eighteen and twenty pounds.'

'It wouldn't be more than she could manage. What're you trying to prove?'

'Just this. Taking it that she carried two cases at a time, she would've had to make four trips from her car to the flat. If she did, it seems more than likely that her neighbour . . . what's the name of the woman in No. 10?'

'Mrs Wentworth.'

'Yes, of course. Well, from what you say, it's logical to expect that this Mrs Wentworth would have heard somebody opening the door of the adjoining flat four times, somebody entering and leaving the flat four times, all within a matter of minutes. Wouldn't you think so?'

'She was certainly curious enough about what went on next door,' Quinn said.

'Yet all she told you was that she saw the kitchen light on

that Wednesday evening and heard Mrs Cooke moving around. She didn't mention a lot of coming and going, did she?'

Quinn combed both hands through his untidy hair. Then he said, 'No . . . and she wouldn't have forgotten a thing like that.'

'So it can't have happened.'

'Evidently not.'

'Right. Now let's go on from there. If the woman who called herself Mrs Cooke visited Hilary Close before driving the car to that garage in St John's Wood, she didn't make four trips up to her flat. Therefore she must've disposed of the money somewhere not far away. Do you agree?'

With a new awareness in his thin peaky face, Quinn said, 'Yes, I do.'

He had a picture in his mind of the route taken by the green Cortina. Earl's Court was the apex of a triangle: Jauncey Engineering . . . Hilary Close . . . Neptune Garage.

Shifting the apex would alter the total distance. And that distance had to tally with the mileage on the speedometer.

Piper asked, 'Any ideas?'

'Well, the choice is rather restricted. Somewhere not far away—some place where a woman could unload eight attaché cases from a car without being noticed—some place where it would be safe to leave fifty-four thousand pounds—some place that she could lock up and always have the key in her possession and—'

Quinn stopped abruptly. With a horsy grin, he asked, 'Are you thinking the same as I'm thinking?'

'Lock-up,' Piper said. 'That's what I've been looking for since yesterday evening. Now it all depends on whether each flat at Hilary Close is provided with a garage.'

'Or even only some of them. If No. 11 has one there's no problem. She could've driven straight in, shut the doors and unloaded the boot in absolute safety. Nobody would've seen a thing.'

'Then all she had to do was reverse out and lock up again. A car driving away wouldn't attract any attention—not enough to make people curious.'

'And certainly not enough to make them associate it later with the robbery at Jauncey Engineering,' Quinn said.

'No, why should they? I wonder . . .'

'What?'

'Most unlikely . . . but it would be funny if the entire payroll was still there, wouldn't it?'

Quinn said, 'I can take that kind of joke. With my share of the reward I'd be laughing all the way to the bank.'

'Why just—' Piper knew the answer but he still had to ask—'just a share? Why shouldn't you have it all to yourself?'

'Because this was a combined effort. Mrs Wentworth shook down the coconut, and I split it open. So each of us is entitled to a third of the milk.'

'Don't be in such a hurry to declare a dividend,' Piper said. 'Right now we don't even know if there is a garage belonging to the flat. We're only guessing.'

'It's a good guess,' Quinn said.

'Perhaps. But that doesn't mean the money was hidden there.'

'Or if it was that it hasn't gone by now. The best way is to go and have a look. What do you say?'

'I don't know. Superintendent Hennant might take a poor view of unofficial snooping.'

'The alternative is to give him the fruits of our mental labours. Is that what you're suggesting?'

'Well, in a way, yes. After all—'

'After all—nuts,' Quinn said.

He held his raincoat open before the fire and swung it to and fro to trap the heat. Then he added, 'If you're scared I'll go alone. But it could cost you eighteen hundred nicker. Think of that.'

Piper said, 'There's something else I'm thinking of. Might provide the motive for what happened to Yvonne Marshall.'

'You mean our idea that she used the garage—if there is a garage?'

'Yes. I still can't understand why Graham stayed away from the flat. He should've been living there since last Wednesday night—but he wasn't. To me that's a mystery I can't get rid of.'

'We don't know that he didn't make a flying visit unbeknown to the nosy Mrs Wentworth.'

'Why just a visit? What's he been doing since Wednesday that stopped him making use of a safe hideout which they'd carefully prepared?'

Quinn shrugged on his coat. He said, 'Don't ask me. Whatever his reason, it's now something that only he can explain. I'm more interested in his motive for throttling the life out of her. Let's hear this thought you had.'

'Nothing very brilliant about it,' Piper said. 'I think money was Graham's motive.'

'Of course it was money! Any fool knows that—including me. I expected a lot better from the master-mind. Money triggered off this whole affair right from the moment . . .'

Quinn swallowed the rest. With a rueful look, he said, 'Don't tell me. I know I'm talking through the back of my neck. You meant motive in a different sense, didn't you?'

'Well, let's call it a restricted sense. My idea is that when he visited the flat yesterday morning he assumed the payroll was there.'

'Because that's where she'd arranged with him to keep it?'

'Yes.'

'In spite of the fact that she'd have had to make umpteen trips up and down the stairs the night she arrived with the eight cases?'

'Perhaps she was supposed to fetch them from the garage one at a time in the next few days.'

'And Graham blew his top when he found she hadn't stuck to the arrangement?'

Piper said, 'It would take more than that to make him behave as he did. I have a feeling things reached a climax for one of two reasons. The more likely is that he'd intended to pick up the fifty-four thousand pounds and go off on his own.'

'Leaving Yvonne high and dry?'

'Yes. Alternatively, she might've had the same intention herself. It could even be that both of them saw no need to share the proceeds.'

'But she couldn't have got away with it if he knew the cases were in the garage.'

'Possibly she made him believe she'd hidden them somewhere else.'

'It's a bit weak,' Quinn said.

'I agree. But I think all the same that the basic situation was near enough as I've put it.'

'You mean Graham killed her because she wouldn't tell him where she'd planted the money?'

'Or he shut her mouth after he'd forced her to tell him.'

'No, I don't get that. He might've had to be rough to get the secret out of her but he didn't have to commit murder. I felt the same way when Sergeant Freeson said they were of the opinion that Graham got rid of her so she couldn't talk.'

Piper said, 'You could be right. If you are, then she died without disclosing the whereabouts of the payroll. In that case, it must still be in the garage.'

'Unless it was never there in the first instance . . . or she really did move it somewhere else.'

'I know a good way to find out.'

'The best way,' Quinn said.

At twenty past ten a taxi dropped them outside Hilary Close. It was still raining but not quite so heavily.

They told the driver to wait. Then they cut across the stretch of lawn.

The centre block had three entrances. A dumpy woman with a shopping basket and an umbrella said the middle one would lead them to the garages at the rear.

'. . . Through that door there. Mind the steps on the other side.'

Melting sleet made the steps treacherous. They led down to a wide concourse with a row of individual garages on two sides and an exit that climbed steeply to road level. Someone had sprinkled sand and gravel the whole length of the slope.

Quinn said, 'They've all got numbers and there would

seem to be one for each flat.'

Several of the double doors were open. There was a car in one garage: others were empty.

No. 11 was shut. Piper said, 'The key's in the lock . . . so I suppose we can take a look. The worst they can do is charge us with trespass—if that.'

'More likely being on enclosed premises with intent,' Quinn said.

The lock was well-oiled, the key turned smoothly. As Piper opened the right-hand door, he said, 'We may not need to go inside.'

With rain pattering on the back of his coat he looked into the garage. The light was poor but he could see brick walls on three sides, a concrete floor, a wooden roof with unfinished rafters. Dead leaves littered the floor and there was a smell of damp.

On the floor close to the end wall lay two large suitcases. They were open and appeared to be empty.

Quinn walked four paces into the garage, paused and looked back. He said, 'And when they got there the cupboard was bare . . . I'll gamble a year's wages the money was in those two cases. Yvonne Marshall must've talked before she died . . . or Mister Graham called her bluff.'

'It's all guesswork,' Piper said.

'One thing isn't. The cash—if it ever was here—has gone. And so has the man who was described as normally good-natured.'

'Perhaps he is like that—normally.'

'Then what made him act subnormally? What turned him into a psychopath? Pinching all the cash for himself should've been enough. He didn't have to kill her that way . . . or any way.'

'If she was his mistress it could be a case of love turning to hate.'

'But why? What could she possibly have done?'

'I don't know. It's possible, however . . .'

'Well, go on.'

'Just suppose—' Piper went far enough into the garage to be beyond reach of the slanting rain—'just suppose Graham discovered that Yvonne had been deceiving him all the time, that she'd used him to obtain a fortune for her and—'

'Now you're going back to my original theory,' Quinn said. 'The police have discarded it and I thought we'd agreed to ignore that business of the useless spare wheel in Graham's car. It's a futile theory now we have proof that Graham must've known all along about this flat in Hilary Close.'

Piper said, 'I'm thinking along different yet parallel lines. Nothing to do with what may have happened to Graham's car at the factory or the idea you told the police. My view is that she didn't mean to trick him until much later.'

'Such as about now?'

'Yes, perhaps. The time doesn't matter. It's the people involved who are important.'

'I only know two,' Quinn said. 'One's in the mortuary: the other's gone into hiding with fifty-four thousand quid to keep him warm. Who else is there?'

'Somebody who had to be in Yvonne Marshall's confidence. Somebody who was kept informed, step by step, right up to the night of the robbery. I may be wrong, of course, but if I'm not, it's a mean sordid affair. Graham was the victim of a conspiracy—not the instigator.'

'And when he found out he killed her,' Quinn said. 'But his real motive wasn't the money they stole from Jauncey Engineering?'

'No. I think there was a greater urge than money. He took the payroll—yes. But I believe he'd have strangled her for what she'd done to him without any other incentive.'

Quinn remembered the question he had been asked by Miss Field and the answer he had given her. It formed a pattern with the events in Flat 11 at Hilary Close.

'... *In his shoes I'd want to make her pay ... and not just for doing me out of my share of the money. It's the other deceit that would hurt me more.*'

He said, 'I don't think you're wrong. There had to be a third party. I felt it in my bones ... but I thought it was flu. Yvonne had another man.'

Piper went out into the rain. Then he turned and said,

'Not just any other man. With someone like Yvonne Marshall it would have to be one particular man. She wasn't a cheap slut.'

'And one particular man doesn't leave us any choice,' Quinn said. 'I doubt if we'll ever prove it. Nor will anybody else. But my nomination is the late Mrs Marshall's bereaved husband.'

CHAPTER XIV

SUPERINTENDENT HENNANT listened politely but he was unimpressed. '. . . This is like the trick of an illusionist who pulls the rabbit out of a hat. There isn't a scrap of evidence to link Marshall with the theft at Jauncey Engineering.'

Quinn said, 'I'm not saying he took part in it. But he and his wife could've taken Graham for a ride. If I'm right he had no come-back. What could he do? Sue her for his share of the stolen money?'

Hennant stood up and walked to the window and looked down at the surging black waters of the Thames. Under Westminster Bridge a heavily-laden barge was fighting its way upriver. On the south bank lights pricked the curtain of rain.

At last, he said, 'You mustn't think I don't appreciate any ideas or suggestions you care to put forward. I can also understand why you visited Hilary Close this morning without consulting me first. Perhaps I was a bit hard on you yesterday.'

'That belongs to the past,' Quinn said. 'I don't bear any ill-will. If I did I wouldn't be here now.'

'Good.' Hennant swung round, his sharp blue eyes quizzical. 'Then tell me what you'd do in my position. Would you arrest Mr Keith Marshall? And, if so, on what charge?'

There was no charge. Quinn knew that only too well. Whatever part Marshall had played he had done nothing that would bring him within reach of the law . . . unless it could be proved.

With Yvonne dead, the only hope of proof had gone. Marshall was safe for all time. His role in the conspiracy would never come to light.

One man alone knew the truth. Even if he were caught, nobody would believe him—nobody would take the word of a thief and a murderer.

. . . Except perhaps his wife. Her faith might be strong enough . . .

Behind the doubt and confusion in Quinn's mind he could hear someone saying, '*. . . I know Harold. Normally he's a good-natured man but he has a temper when he's roused.*'

Quinn said, 'I realize, Superintendent, that you've got no evidence against Marshall. All I'm trying to suggest is that Graham didn't have merely a financial motive for killing Yvonne Marshall.'

Hennant plucked at his protruding lower lip. Then he put both hands behind his back and swayed to and fro.

He said, 'What real difference does it make? Can you see any jury accepting in mitigation that he was emotionally disturbed because his partner in crime and her husband had conned him?'

'No, of course not. I just don't like the idea of Marshall getting away with it.'

'Getting away with what? He's not only lost his wife but fifty-four thousand pounds into the bargain. Assuming he is a crook—and that's assuming a lot—he hasn't exactly shown a profit on the deal, has he?'

Quinn said, 'Everything you say is true. I wouldn't dream of arguing.'

'Then what's worrying you? What is this bee you've got in your bonnet?'

'I don't know. You may think I'm crazy . . . but there's something about this whole affair right from the start that isn't—well, call it logical.'

'Does it have to be?' Hennant shook his head. 'Human behaviour seldom conforms to the rules of logic. The psychiatrists say no one commits murder unless he's off his rocker, anyway. In Graham's case, his life must've become so topsy-turvy that it wouldn't take much to push him over the edge. We'll find out whether he's legally sane or not when we catch him.'

'Do you think you'll ever get close enough?'

'With a measure of luck—maybe. We'll have more chance if we don't clutter up our minds with wild notions . . . if you don't mind my saying so.'

Quinn said, 'Why should I mind? When I can't even convince myself, what right have I to expect you to understand?'

'Well, I have tried.'

'Yes, I must admit you have. In fact, you've been very patient.'

'It's one virtue more than any other that you learn in my job,' Hennant said. 'However . . .'

He looked up at the big electric clock on the wall. As he came back to his desk, he asked, 'Anything else I can do for you, Mr Quinn?'

'No, I don't think so. It's time I took myself off before I overstay my welcome.'

Once again, Quinn could hear Miss Field's troubled voice—the phrase that stuck in his mind: '. . . *Normally good-natured . . . normally good-natured . . .*'

He got out of his chair and went to the door. Then he said, 'You know, I feel almost sorry for Harold Graham. That shows you how crazy I am.'

'Why should you feel sorry for him?'

'Because, as I see it, he's a man who just disintegrated under the weight of circumstances.'

'What circumstances? He had a good job—'

'—which he had reason to believe wouldn't last long. I suppose you know about the take-over bid for Jauncey Engineering?'

'No. Who told you about it?'

'A friend of mine called Piper. He got it from Mrs Graham.'

Superintendent Hennant looked thoughtful. He said, 'I shouldn't imagine a man in Graham's position would have any cause to worry.'

'When there's a take-over nobody's secure,' Quinn said. 'The higher they are the harder they fall.'

'Wasn't he on contract?'

'Evidently not. According to his wife, the prospect worried them sick. Graham knew what we all know—in spite of the usual flannel when one company swallows up another.'

'All the same, it doesn't justify robbing his firm,' Hennant said.

'Obviously, he thought it did. By way of compensation for the anticipated loss of his job he took his own golden handshake. Against the law, of course . . . but our modern commercial jungle is no place for fine principles. How would you like to work conscientiously for nine years and then be tossed on to the labour market when you were over forty-five?'

The question seemed to amuse Superintendent Hennant. He said, 'You sound as if you'd been a victim of big business yourself.'

'Not me. But I've seen it all happen time and time again. And always the same story—nobody's job is at risk. Whenever I read that, I don't give the poor devils more than six to twelve months.'

'And you think this is what preyed on Graham's mind?'

'I'm sure of it. His wife goes as far as to say she hardly blames him. She knew what he was dreading: after the take-over honeymoon comes the night of the long knives.'

'You're exaggerating,' Hennant said. 'It isn't always like that.'

'Oh, but it is, more often than not. Graham foresaw the inevitable reorganization, rationalization, centralization, computerization, almagamation, assimilation—all the claptrap which adds up to the same thing in the end. And it is the end.'

'You'd make—' the superintendent's alert blue eyes were no longer amused—'a pretty good advocate for him.'

Quinn said, 'Not just for him. Take-overs are my pet hobby-horse. I've felt for years that when accountants come

in through the door humanity goes out through the window
... to paraphrase an old saying.'

A sudden frown deepened the lines in Hennant's face. He asked, 'How much humanity would you say there was in a man who strangled his mistress?'

'That's what I can't understand,' Quinn said.

As he opened the door, he added, 'I'll never understand.'

He had a sandwich and a glass of bitter in the Royal Duke —a busy pub not far from Westminster Abbey. There was no one he knew in the lounge bar and he was left alone with his thoughts.

For a long time he sat building a castle of ideas ... and knocking it down ... and building another ... and another. Over his second bitter he came to the conclusion that the castle would never stand up because the foundations were wrong.

And at last he saw what he told himself he should have seen when he and Piper talked together outside the garage at Hilary Close. They had been very near—but not near enough.

When he switched the relationship between Yvonne Marshall and her husband and Harold Graham the pattern of events became a logical pattern. His mistake had been in getting them wrong way round.

Marshall—not Graham. If Marshall had not been told what his wife and Graham were plotting ... if Marshall had found out for himself ... if Marshall had learned that Yvonne would go into hiding at Hilary Court ... if Marshall had decided to rid himself of an unfaithful wife and gain a fortune at the same time ...

The castle stood firm against every assault. Now it was all very simple.

One thing only was still unexplained. And that was trivial compared with the death of Yvonne Marshall.

Her husband would scarcely have troubled to provide himself with an alibi for the time she was murdered. He had no need. Graham would be blamed. Graham, the absconding cashier, would be blamed for everything.

From the call box in the Royal Duke, Quinn phoned Scotland Yard and asked Hennant if he knew the name of Keith Marshall's employers. '... I didn't think he'd be at home this hour of the day but I tried all the same a couple of minutes ago.'

'And?'

'No reply. His firm may know how I can get in touch with him so if you'd tell me who they are . . .'

'Why do you want him?'

'Just to ask one or two discreet questions.'

Superintendent Hennant said, 'See they are discreet. Better still, make sure you and Marshall are alone before you say something you might regret.'

'Don't worry. I'll be the soul of discretion.'

'If you're not, you and your paper could be on the losing end of a slander action.'

'Don't I know?'

'All right,' Hennant said. 'It's your own lookout. He works for Hill and Makin, roofing contractors, Wembley Industrial Estate.'

Quinn was transferred from one department to another until a man in Sales told him Mr Marshall was out of town. '... He'll be in South Wales the whole of this week. Anything I can do?'

'No, it's a personal matter. I arranged to phone him and I haven't had a moment until now. When did he leave town?'

'Today.'

'Oh, so he's got his car back?'

'Yes, picked it up on Saturday. You know about his wife, I suppose?'

'Bad business,' Quinn said. 'He's been kicked around a lot in the past week.'

'You can say that again. Best thing for him is to be back at work. Take his mind off it.'

'Well, it'll help, anyway. Did he leave early?'

'No, he had some things to clear up first. Called in here before he left.'

'What time would that be?'

'Between half-eleven and twelve. Why?'

'Just a passing thought,' Quinn said. 'He told me he'd be going off yesterday and I was thinking it was as well he didn't. The police needed him to identify his wife.'

'Yes, I know. Must've been a nasty experience. As it happens he was in and out of the office all day and they were able to get hold of him pretty quickly.'

The line whistled and crackled and several voices overlapped each other. Then the man at the other end was saying, '. . . give me your name, I'll tell him you rang. He'll probably be phoning us tomorrow.'

Quinn said, 'My name's Graham—Harold Graham. You can say he'll be hearing from me again.'

There was no reply from the house in Maryland Avenue. Either Mrs Graham had gone out or she was not answering the phone. If she were at home, Quinn could understand that she would not be anxious to talk to people after the events at Hilary Close.

He remembered the look on Marshall's heavy face when they discussed Graham's wife: '. . . *Damn shame . . . What does a woman do when her husband goes off with somebody else?*'

Then he had repeated, '*Damn shame . . .*'

Miss Field's number was one of many scribbled in Quinn's tattered note-book. While he was searching through it, someone opened the door of the phone box and asked, 'Will you be long?'

'No, only a couple of minutes. Just got a quick call to make.'

'Well, keep it short, mate. I want to put a bet on the three o'clock.'

The door swung shut again as Quinn found the number. He wondered if Miss Field would believe him. She might think it was just another newspaperman's trick to badger her sister.

Whatever she thought he had to try. She would know how he could get in touch with Mrs Graham. She could persuade Mrs Graham to listen to him.

The phone went on ringing for a long time. Then a youthful voice answered.

'... Hold the line, please. I'll put you through.'

Again he had a long wait. The man outside the box was becoming impatient.

Just when Quinn had decided that he must have been cut off, a different voice said, 'Barbara Field. Who is that?'

'Quinn ... *Morning Post*. Remember me?'

'Yes, of course. But I never expected to hear from you.'

'Why not? You gave me your phone number and I said I'd ring you if anything new turned up.'

'That was before—' she faltered and went on awkwardly —'before what happened yesterday.'

'Well, wouldn't you say that was new?'

'Yes, but I don't want to talk about it. So if you'll excuse me—'

'Sounds as if you've already made up your mind that your brother-in-law did it,' Quinn said.

In a changed tone, she asked, 'What do you mean by that? Who else could it have been?'

'If you'll meet me at your sister's house I'll tell you.'

'Why does she have to be subjected to any more distress? Don't you think she's suffered enough?'

'More than enough,' Quinn said. 'But I need her co-operation. She knows better than anyone whether her husband could do what everybody is so convinced he has done.'

'Does it matter? After the way he treated her do you think she cares what happens to him?'

'Yes, I do. She still looks on herself as his wife. And she's admitted she doesn't really blame him for robbing the Company. She says he was driven to it by the threat of a take-over bid.'

'Who told you all this?'

'An insurance assessor I know. He called on your sister recently.'

'What did he want?'

'To talk about insurance, I presume.'

After a little silence, Barbara Field said, 'She didn't tell me. I wonder why?'

'Probably thought it wasn't important. She has other things on her mind. And that's where I want to help. I wasn't kidding when I said I had a personal interest in this affair. Remember?'

'Yes. And you really do think Harold didn't—didn't kill that woman?'

'It's my belief he had nothing to do with it. To be frank, I wouldn't have bothered you if I could've spoken to your sister personally . . . but I couldn't get her on the phone.'

'No, she doesn't want to speak to anyone. But this is different. You may do her some good. She's in such a state of depression I'm not sure she should be left on her own.'

'The past five days have been enough to shatter any woman,' Quinn said.

'You just can't realize what they've done to her. She blames herself for what's happened . . . stupid though it may be. I can't make her see it wasn't her fault.'

'Maybe I'll manage to put things in the right perspective for her,' Quinn said.

'I hope so . . . I do hope so.'

The man outside was making impatient gestures. Quinn saw him point to his watch and hold up three fingers.

Then Barbara Field asked, 'When would you like to come to the house?'

'Any time to suit you.'

'Well, I'm going there straight from the office. Is six-thirty all right?'

'Six-thirty will be fine. But there's just one thing . . .'

'Yes?'

'Don't tell your sister I'm coming,' Quinn said. 'In fact, don't even mention that I've spoken to you.'

He rang Piper's office but the number was engaged. After he had tried a second time he told himself that what he had to say would keep.

... Plenty of time to show him what a clever little boy you are. Can't beat the old touch of genius ... if you're right. Maybe you shouldn't be so quick to throw your non-existent hat in the air. All the same, you must be right. It's the only answer which fits all the facts ...

It was nearly three o'clock. Just time to have a pint. Last he would get before he visited Crouch End. Never do to be smelling of drink when he called on the deserted wife of a man who was wanted for murder.

CHAPTER XV

MRS GRAHAM WAS VERY MUCH as Piper had described her: a little woman, small-boned and with dark hair and dark eyes. They were the tired eyes of someone who had been under continual strain.

She looked at Quinn without interest when Barbara Field introduced him. He knew it was going to be difficult to get through the wall of apathy.

'... I told Mr Quinn you were in no mood for visitors, Ethel, but he convinced me he has certain information which should make you feel better. In your own interests I think you should listen to him.'

'What information—' Mrs Graham glanced at Quinn and then turned away—'what information can you have that will make any difference to what they say Harold has done? Nothing can change that. Stealing was bad enough but this ...' She wrapped one hand in the other and put them to her mouth.

Quinn said, 'You don't have to believe what anybody says about your husband. It's my opinion he wasn't responsible for the death of Yvonne Marshall.'

'Then who killed her? Who else would want to kill her?'

'That's something I'd rather not discuss right now. I'm only here to ask you a question that you alone can answer

'. . . if you will.'

Mrs Graham raised her head slowly. In the same dull voice, she asked, 'What is your question?'

'It's not very difficult. But I'd like you to be honest with me.'

'Honest?' Her mouth drooped plaintively. 'After what my husband did last Wednesday night do you expect to get an honest answer in this house?'

Barbara Field said, 'Please, Ethel. I've told you again and again that it wasn't your fault. None of it was your fault. Mr Quinn's trying to help. You must take a hold of yourself.'

There was a note of reprimand in her voice. Quinn guessed it was not the first time she had lost patience with her sister.

They were two different types: different in temperament, different in looks. Barbara was strong and reliable. Ethel was the kind of woman who would inevitably yield under pressure. That might explain why her marriage had crumbled when the stress became too great.

He said, 'Look, Mrs Graham. It'll be better all round if we talk straight. Your husband's a thief. There can be no argument about that. Maybe you can make excuses for him, maybe I don't blame him, either. But the fact of the matter is that he stole a large sum of money from his employers.'

'Only because—' a momentary touch of spirit showed in Ethel Graham's drawn face—'only because that woman put him up to it. I don't hate her any more now she's dead . . . but I know my husband. He'd never have done a thing like that all by himself. She must've been at him for months . . . she must've been. I know him only too well.'

'That's why I'm here,' Quinn said. 'I want you to tell me if your husband could possibly have committed murder—whatever the provocation.'

She looked at him, her dark sad eyes suddenly wide and questioning. She said, 'You really don't believe he killed her . . . do you?'

'No, I don't. In my job I've met many thieves—professional thieves—and the vast majority of them wouldn't hurt a living soul. So let's separate what happened last Wednesday night from what happened yesterday morning. Stealing isn't killing. One thing has nothing to do with another. Will you fix your mind on that, Mrs Graham?'

'Yes . . . oh, yes, I will.' She turned to her sister. 'Harold's a kind man. You know that. He's never hurt anyone in his life, has he?'

Barbara Field said, 'Not in that way. I don't think he could ever use violence . . . unless he's gone off his head. But he has hurt you. And that's what I can't forgive.'

'Only because you don't realize the amount of worry he's had in the past five or six months. I never told you the firm was going to be taken over . . . he asked me not to. Day and night he lived with the fear that he'd lose his job. And you know how hard he worked to become chief cashier, don't you?'

The look in Barbara's warm brown eyes softened. In a changed tone, she said, 'Yes, I do. It's a great shame . . . after all these years. Perhaps I was wrong about him and that woman Marshall. Perhaps he only needed her to help him open . . .'

Her voice tailed off. Then she looked at Quinn and asked, 'Are you still convinced they weren't lovers?'

For a moment he was tempted. But it made no difference now whether he told the truth or not. Nobody cared any longer what Yvonne Marshall had been—least of all Yvonne Marshall.

Only one person knew if she had been his mistress. If he were never caught it would be his secret for all time.

To leave Ethel Graham with a crumb of comfort cost nothing. She had already suffered enough.

Quinn said, 'Yes. I think they were merely partners in the theft of Jauncey's payroll. It's more than possible he'd have sent for his wife when he found a place of safety.'

Barbara Field knew he was lying. He could see it in her face. But she must also have known his reason.

She said, 'If that's true, Harold had no motive for killing Mrs Marshall.'

'Not a strong enough motive—even if she tried to cheat

him out of his share of the money.'

Mrs Graham sat up straight and leaned forward. She asked, 'Did—did that woman have all of it?'

'When she left the factory—yes,' Quinn said. 'There seems little doubt about that. On Wednesday night she drove from the factory to her flat in Earl's Court and hid the money there. As I see it your husband was supposed to collect his share later.'

'Do you mean he didn't?'

'Yes. It's only my idea and the police don't agree . . . but I think someone else visited the flat yesterday, killed Mrs Marshall to stop her talking and made off with the fifty-four thousand pounds she'd hidden in the garage.'

'But who—' Mrs Graham looked lost and bewildered—'who could've known she was living there?'

Quinn said, 'If I told you whom I suspect I might land myself in a lot of trouble. Let's leave that part for the time being. The main thing is that you don't believe your husband was responsible for what happened yesterday morning.'

'No, I don't. Not any more. I was so confused I didn't know what to believe. Now I'm quite sure he couldn't have done it . . . quite, quite sure.'

'Good. My journey hasn't been in vain.'

In a hesitant voice, Barbara Field said, 'I know you really are trying to help my sister and I'm sorry I was rude to you the other day . . . but how will you get the police to accept your ideas about this other person?'

'There's a straight answer to that,' Quinn said. 'I don't know.'

'So if they arrest Harold they'll charge him with murder.'

'Providing they think they can make it stick. If they can't, they'll certainly get a conviction for the theft of Jauncey's payroll. It might not make all that much difference to the length of time your brother-in-law serves. From his point of view it hardly matters what he's convicted of.'

'But it matters to my sister. There may be some excuse for stealing but not for murder. Haven't you any way of proving it was somebody else?'

'Not right now. All I can promise is that I'll work at it.'

Ethel Graham watched him stand up and fasten his raincoat. Then she held out her small fine-boned hand to him.

With a brighter look in her eyes, she said, 'I want you to know how grateful I am. I'd lost faith in everything. But you and Barbara have made me see I must—'

Her voice broke. She let go of his hand and turned away and he saw tears come into her eyes.

Barbara walked with him to the front door. As he was going out, she said, 'I don't want you to tell me who this other person is. It wouldn't be fair . . . and I think I can guess, anyway. Only somebody who hated Mrs Marshall could've killed her. It wasn't for the money, was it?'

Quinn said, 'No . . . not for the money alone. My guess is it acted as an additional incentive—but that was all.'

He wanted to say many things to this girl with the soft brown eyes and hair like spun gold. It had been a long time since anyone had looked at him as she was looking at him now. Yet he knew he ran the risk of making a damn fool of himself.

. . . What on earth do you imagine she sees in you? Just because she isn't married doesn't mean she'll fancy the first tramp who gets ideas about her. All she's thinking of is her sister. If Ethel's grateful, Barbara's pleased. No more than that. Don't get any notion that she looks on you as a knight in shining armour . . .

But the temptation lingered. It grew stronger when she said, 'I wasn't very nice to you last time you were here and I'd like to apologize. My only excuse is that I was terribly worried about my sister.'

'It's quite natural,' Quinn said. 'I don't blame you for being short with a stranger who barged in when you had a lot on your mind.'

She smiled as she gave him her hand. It was a pretty smile. Her hand was smooth and warm and the street light outside the gate put stars in her eyes.

In a small voice, she said, 'It's nice of you to say that. And thank you for being so kind to Ethel. As I told you on the phone I've been scared of what she might do.'

He had a sudden heady sensation as though he had been drinking. When it cleared, he said, 'After this is all over and done with do you think we might meet somewhere one night when you've got an hour to spare? Maybe do a show or have a meal or whatever you fancied.'

'Why not?' She seemed to have forgotten he was still holding her hand. 'It would be very pleasant if we just sat and talked.'

'Yes, I'd like that, too,' Quinn said.

He released her fingers and stepped back awkwardly and almost tripped over his own feet. He had never felt like this in his whole life. No girl had ever had such an effect on him.

And she was just an ordinary girl. Nothing special to look at. Some men might not even call her attractive.

Yet to him she was very special. They had met only twice and he knew nothing about her but she was the one he had thought he would never find.

... Funny how things happen. If two people I'd never heard of a week ago hadn't stolen a fortune from Jauncey Engineering last Wednesday night I wouldn't be standing here like a romantic teenager who doesn't know how to say goodbye. Just as well you got a haircut yesterday morning ...

As though the shutter of a projector in his mind had opened he could see the bloated discoloured face of a woman who had died with a stocking tied viciously round her neck. She might have lived if he had not gone for a haircut.

Funny how things happened . . . But not so funny for Yvonne Marshall.

Then Barbara gave him a little wave and began to close the door. He wanted to tell her he would phone to make a date for his first night off but he was afraid. It might sound too hasty.

There was plenty of time . . . plenty of time. No need to rush. The mood might pass. Give her the chance to change her mind.

Barbara said, 'Goodnight . . . and thank you again for

being so nice to my sister.'

The door closed with a tiny click of the latch. Her footsteps receded along the hall. Light spilled out momentarily as another door opened and shut again.

After that Quinn found himself outside the gate with no recollection of how he got there. The haunting picture of a dead woman had vanished. All he could think of was Barbara's smile and the stars in her eyes.

On Wednesday morning he phoned Piper. They talked around the subject of Keith Marshall without coming to any conclusion but Quinn was left with the impression that Piper's attitude had changed slightly.

'... I've been asking myself how he got into the flat. He couldn't have had a key ... so his wife would've had to let him in.'

'Well, she wouldn't know who it was until she opened the door. And it would be too late then to stop him.'

'What you're saying is that he forced his way in and the attack was so sudden she didn't have the chance to scream or make any kind of noise that would've attracted attention.'

'More or less.'

'But there was bound to be some noise. She must've put up a struggle.'

'She did,' Quinn said. 'The back of her dress was ripped apart and her nails were all split.'

'So you mentioned. That's what has been worrying me. If she were attacked and killed immediately she opened the door she wouldn't have been strangled from behind. If she managed to turn and run she'd have been able to scream for help before the nylon was put round her neck.'

'Maybe he got the stocking over her head as soon as she turned her back on him. There'd have been no time to scream.'

Piper said, 'That would mean he got her face down on the floor only a yard or so from the doorway. The whole thing must've taken place right there.'

'It would appear so ... although I can see a flaw in that

without having to be told. If she died in the hall—'

'Why wasn't her body left there instead of being dragged or carried into the spare bedroom?'

'I don't know,' Quinn said. 'I hadn't thought of that before.'

'Then here's something else to think about. How could she have been killed in the hall? From what you described to me, all the signs were that she died in the spare room. The position of her hands, the posture of her body—everything indicates that it must have happened there. Don't you agree?'

'Oh, but yes. And now you've got me worried.'

'Better that than to be misled by appearances. Incidentally, you did say she'd been struck on the head, didn't you?'

'Yes . . . according to the police surgeon. Not a serious blow but enough to knock her half-silly.'

'Where was she hit?'

'A little below the crown of the head.'

'So again she must've been attacked from behind. And before she recovered from the blow he strangled her. That should mean she was struck down as soon as she saw who it was and turned to run.'

'But she died in the spare room,' Quinn said.

Two conflicting sets of facts . . . Both valid yet both contradictory. Therefore the truth lay between the two.

Piper said, 'While she was trying to escape from the man who'd forced his way into her flat she'd make a row . . . like any woman would when faced with imminent death. But she couldn't have tried to escape—or got very far—because she received a blow on the head. And then she was strangled. Yet she died in the spare room.'

'Now the answer's a lemon,' Quinn said.

'In more ways than one. Even supposing she didn't scream while she ran . . . why run into the spare room? And why turn her back when she got there so that he could hit her on the back of the head?'

'I don't know. But I have a feeling you do.'

'Well, I'm willing to make a guess. Suppose she didn't have to open the front door to let him in? Suppose he had a key . . . and she was in the spare room for some reason that isn't important now . . . and he crept up behind her and knocked her semi-conscious? How does it look now?'

'Plausible—distinctly plausible. And once again we've travelled full-circle. We're back to Harold Graham. He'd have a key to the flat.'

'Marshall could've had one as well,' Piper said.

'How?'

'He could have got it from his wife.'

'Meaning they'd planned all along to slip it across Yvonne's gullible boy-friend?'

'Yes. It's still as good a theory as any I can think of.'

Quinn said, 'Round and round the mulberry bush. If she and her crooked hubby were in it together she wouldn't suspect he wanted the whole fifty-four thousand for himself. So she wouldn't be scared of him. In other words he could've got her into the spare room on some pretext. But that also applies to Harold Graham . . . right?'

'Only one criticism. Why the spare room?'

'How should I know? It's your idea that either of them could've had a key.'

'No more than a guess,' Piper said. 'Whichever one it was, I'm pretty sure of this: he came equipped with a nylon stocking. She had the keys to the garage and the only way to get his hands on them was to eliminate Yvonne.'

'You're wrong there. The only way for her husband but not for Graham. Marshall would be afraid she'd shop him but Graham didn't have that worry. He's already on the run. He didn't have to kill her to make sure she couldn't talk.'

'So once again it seems Yvonne Marshall died because somebody wanted her dead—and that somebody must have been Keith Marshall.'

'There's no must about it. I tried that concept on Superintendent Hennant and he sent me off with a flea in my ear. His money's on Graham.'

'How does Hennant account for the twin beds and twin wardrobes and so on?'

'He doesn't. I think he believes all the answers will pop

up when he lays his hands on Jauncey's absconding cashier.'

Piper said, 'Robbery and murder in one neat parcel. But neither Mrs Graham nor her sister consider that he could ever resort to violence. Wonder if they are right?'

'We'll know when the police find him . . . if they find him. He'll either have the money or he won't. If he's never had it he didn't kill Yvonne.'

'Don't be too dogmatic. There's a flaw somewhere in all our reasoning. Haven't you felt it?'

'Right from the start,' Quinn said. 'We've left something out. Until we know what it is we'll always get the wrong answer.'

CHAPTER XVI

IT RAINED almost non-stop all day Wednesday and throughout the night. Then the wind shifted from west to north-east. By noon on Thursday the sky had cleared and wintry sunshine was drying the streets.

Just before Superintendent Hennant broke off for lunch he received another report that someone had seen a man resembling Harold Graham. That made eight.

This time the report came from Cornwall. The others had been spread over the Home Counties with the exception of one from Birmingham. All were found to be without substance.

The latest report seemed more promising. The man who answered Graham's description had stayed overnight at a small hotel in Truro. He had been accompanied by a woman—ostensibly his wife—and they were understood to be on their way to St Ives.

It was the wife of the hotel manager who claimed that the man was Graham. By the time she notified the local police he and the woman had gone. Regional crime squad were treating the information seriously.

Hennant said to himself, 'Maybe . . . maybe not. I think not.'

During lunch he had transient recollections of what had happened at Jauncey Engineering works on the evening of November 4. When he came back to his office he separated the patrolman's story into its component parts and studied them from an oblique angle.

Reg Tugwell had given a coherent account of what he had been told by the head cashier and Mrs Marshall and what he had witnessed personally. But the whole thing was a subjective impression of events seen through the eyes of one man—a man who had been knocked unconscious the moment he rushed into Mrs Marshall's office. The question was how long he had been unconscious.

When the police questioned him it was taken for granted that he woke up after the two getaway cars had driven away from the factory. He said he could hear the noise of passing traffic. No one had asked him if some of that noise might not have been the departure of Harold Graham's Hillman or Mrs Marshall's hired Cortina . . . leaving singly or together.

If both of them had left at the same time, then Graham might well have discovered he had a flat tyre on his way to the docks. The delay would not have been important. Ten minutes more or less made no difference to the schedule he had set himself.

There the superintendent wondered if any reliance could be placed on Tugwell's memory of events immediately before and after he had been struck down. Some form of amnesia often existed prior to or following an injury to the head. Frequently it occurred during both periods.

Yet it was also possible that he now remembered more than he could recall on the morning of November 5. If he were able to say whether he had heard one car . . . or two cars together . . . or two cars with an interval between them . . .

Hennant was asked to hold the line while Personnel Department made inquiries. It seemed a long time before the phone said, 'Tugwell has only done one spell of duty since that business Wednesday evening. He was on night shift Saturday and went off nine a.m. Sunday morning. Hasn't been seen since then.'

'That's four days ago. Any reason why he should've stayed off work?'

'Well, you might call it a reason. We list it as compensationitis. He's been suffering from real bad headaches as a result of the knock he got . . . so he says. A fat cheque from the insurance will probably effect one of those miraculous cures you read about in the Scriptures.'

'Don't you check up on employees when they're off as long as this?'

'Not Reg Tugwell. We know what's wrong with him. Apart from which, employees are supposed to get in touch with us when they don't show up for work. It's not our business to chase after them. Would you like his address?'

'I've already got it,' Hennant said. 'Thanks all the same.'

Someone mentioned the phone call to the works manager while he was inspecting the site of the new factory building. He said, 'If they want Tugwell they know where to find him. Shouldn't have thought he could tell Scotland Yard any more than he's already told them . . . but that's their affair. Anyone needs me I'll be here for the next half-hour or thereabouts.'

As he squelched around, his rubber boots ankle-deep in mud, he was idly thinking about the patrol staff. Then something more immediate pushed the thought out of his mind.

After days of almost continuous rain the site was waterlogged. No construction work had been done since Monday. Caterpillar tracks in the clay were like criss-crossing moats and the new stretch of roadway was flooded a foot deep.

Part of the scaffolding had sunk in the soggy earth and needed reinforcing. A mound of sand had been nearly washed away. He made a note to find out why it had not been protected with plastic sheets.

Two pumps were lowering the level of water in a trench where power cables had been laid. A man in thigh boots had clambered down to make sure the intake hoses were kept free of obstruction. Up above, another man with a shovel scraped a channel for the outflow to escape.

Above the noise of the pumps, the works manager asked, 'When were these things started?'

'A couple of hours ago, sir.'

'Why did you wait till then? What was wrong with first thing this morning?'

'Nothing to do with me, sir. We get our orders from the foreman.'

'Where is he?'

'Somewhere around, I expect. Do you want to see him?'

The works manager said, 'I do—and right now.'

He stood watching the motor-driven pumps discharging yellow muddy water in rhythmic spurts like the pulsing of two severed arteries. The level in the trench had begun to fall and part of the cable could now be seen. It was half-buried under a mound of soil that had eroded from one of the side walls.

Cracks showed in the opposite wall where a section bulged under the pressure of drainage from higher ground. The man down below waded closer, took a long look and called out, 'Doesn't strike me that this'll hold, sir. If we're going to make a final inspection of the cable we'll have to put up some shuttering or the whole damn lot is likely to—'

He stopped. Then he used his hands to shift some lumps of clay just below the surface of the water.

A moment later he backed away and stared up with a shocked look in his eyes. He said, 'You'd better get the police, sir. There's somebody buried down here . . .'

Screens were erected and the trench pumped almost free of water. Superintendent Hennant and the police surgeon watched while two men, working slowly and carefully, cleared away fallen earth and gravel until the body was completely exposed.

Hennant said, 'Now it's all yours, doctor. I'm not expecting you to tell me very much. If you can state time and cause of death that'll do for a start. I'm more interested in identification.'

The police surgeon used a ladder to get down and his equipment was lowered to him at the end of a rope. For a minute or two he worked in silence.

Then he complained, 'I can't possibly carry out an examination in these conditions. I'm plastered in mud already. To tackle the job properly I need a trestle table. See what you can do, Superintendent.'

The works manager provided a table and the body was brought up. With extra screens shielding him from the wind the doctor began his task again.

At the end of twenty minutes he rejoined Hennant. '. . . This is as much as I can tell you pending a full-scale post-mortem. The deceased is a man of about forty, perhaps a little older: average height: dark hair with a touch of grey: well-preserved teeth: brown eyes. Does that description mean anything to you?'

'It's familiar,' Hennant said. 'How did he die?'

'Well, provisionally, I'd say he drowned. Appearances seem to indicate that he fell head first into the trench which may have contained several inches of water at the time. There is a bruise on the top of the skull that could have been caused when he landed on his head. I found two or three lumps of sandstone in the mud at the bottom.'

'You don't think he could've died from the blow on the head?'

'No, I doubt it. Have to wait for the PM of course, but my opinion is that he was knocked unconscious long enough to drown. I found a quantity of water in his lungs. If the trench had been dry he may well have survived the fall.'

Hennant said, 'If it was a fall in the normal sense. Any chance he was hit on the head and then thrown into the pit . . . like Joseph of old?'

'Not a good analogy,' the doctor said. 'I don't recall that Joseph was other than fully conscious when his brothers disposed of him.'

'All right . . . forget the Children of Israel. Is it possible that this fellow was knocked out first?'

'Anything's possible. But I'm not paid to guess. I only tell you what I find.'

'OK. I'm satisfied. How long has he been dead?'

'Well, that's not easy to establish with any degree of certainty. We've had cold weather of late but conditions below ground are not so cold. Against that he was lying in water . . . but not running water. Presents quite a problem, in fact.'

'Adding up to what? I'm only asking for a rough estimation.'

'And that's all you're going to get. Judging by the amount of discoloration and swelling of the neck and face, decomposition of the trunk well established, all the signs are . . . let me see.'

He ticked off detail by detail on his fingers while he thought. Then he said, 'In my opinion, not less than five to six days . . . and possibly longer.'

'As long ago as a week last night?'

'Yes, quite likely.'

Superintendent Hennant said, 'I'm much obliged.'

The works manager and a technical director jointly identified the body. '. . . He's damned unpleasant to look at but that's Harold Graham.'

'You're absolutely sure?'

Both of them said they were positive. The works manager asked, 'Has he been there all the time?'

'So it would appear.'

'You mean since the night the payroll was taken?'

'Probably.'

'Have you any idea how it happened?'

'Lots of ideas,' Hennant said. 'All I have to do now is sort out one that I can prove.'

Quinn heard the news late that afternoon. He tried to speak to Superintendent Hennant or alternatively Sergeant Freeson on the telephone but neither of them was available.

So he rang Piper. '. . . Nearly all the answers. Graham found he had a flat tyre and stayed behind to put on the spare while Mrs Marshall went off to plant the stolen money. She must've been in a flap when he didn't show up at Hilary Close that night.'

'Or the next day,' Piper said. 'I can imagine how she felt as the days went by and he still hadn't got in touch with her.'

'Yes, they'd made plans for everything but that. Now we know why there were twin beds, two bedside tables and reading lamps, two wardrobes. A complete love-nest—complete with fifty-four thousand pounds in the garage.'

'And a woman who would've exchanged it all for the chance to go back to the morning of Wednesday, November 4,' Piper said.

In his mind's eye Quinn could see an image of Yvonne Marshall, frightened and alone and with no one in whom she could confide, waiting day after day for the man she would never see again, the man who had been meant to make the whole affair worthwhile. And then death brought release from the interminable waiting—death in the empty loneliness of Flat No. 11.

He said, 'My information is that Graham may have died by falling into the hole where they'd laid an electricity cable. Seems he could have hit his head on a piece of rock.'

'Or a piece of rock could have hit him on the head. He had no reason at all to be there.'

'None that we know of. I'd say it's much more likely he got clobbered when he was changing the spare wheel. Then somebody dragged him from outside Admin to the building site and pushed him over the edge of the hole.'

'Where his body might have lain for years or perhaps for ever if heavy rainfall hadn't flooded the trench and uncovered him. Except for that, the police would have gone on hunting for Harold Graham while somebody else enjoyed the proceeds of the robbery.'

'Only after Mrs Marshall was eliminated,' Quinn said.

'Not necessarily. The more I think about it the more I'm convinced her death was a separate issue. She could have been knocked out, the garage keys taken and the money removed without interference. But evidently that wasn't enough.'

'Perhaps she had to die because she'd seen her killer.'

'Or perhaps because that was the reward of betrayal.'

'Now we're back to her sorrowing husband.'

'Maybe. If Marshall killed his wife, then he must have been responsible for Graham's death. What happened at the Jauncey Engineering works was deliberate. The attack on Graham came from behind. He couldn't have seen his assailant . . . so he didn't have to die.'

'But he did,' Quinn said. 'I think one of the answers is still missing. Marshall should've wanted his wife's lover to stay alive.'

'Why?'

'Poetic justice. Cast your mind back to what happened that night. If Keith Marshall got into the factory somehow, he'd know the patrolman had been put to sleep because he'd interrupted the thieves . . . which meant he could identify them. Do you follow my train of thought?'

Piper said, 'Yes. Graham should have been left to get on with changing the spare wheel—'

'Marshall having let down one of the rear tyres.'

'Probably. With Graham out of the way, there was nothing to stop Marshall from following his wife to Hilary Close, disposing of her and then going off with the payroll.'

'Leaving lover-boy to carry the can,' Quinn said. 'Glad you see it like I do. Graham could proclaim his innocence to high heaven but nobody would believe him. He'd be done for robbery and murder. If I'd been Marshall that would've made the fifty-four thousand quid taste even sweeter.'

'But events didn't turn out that way,' Piper said.

'No. So either he panicked—'

'Which I very much doubt.'

'Me, too. The only alternative, therefore, is that it wasn't Keith Marshall wot done it but somebody else who got wise to what was going on and . . . and . . .'

Quinn's voice dwindled away. Then he had a bout of coughing.

When he recovered his breath, he said, 'One of these days my chest is going to get me into trouble . . . as the actress said to the bishop. What was I saying before I was took bad with me tubes?'

'You were suggesting that it wasn't Keith Marshall but somebody else.'

'Was I? Oh, yes . . .' His voice faded again.

Piper asked, 'Are you deep in thought or has your mind gone blank?'

'That's a good question. The answer is a bit of both.'

'What do you mean by that?'

After another long silence, Quinn said, 'I've just had an idea—the daftest idea you could ever imagine. If there's anything in it, I'm a genius.'

'Why not let me judge? Or do you want to keep it to yourself in case it's as daft as you think it might be?'

'No, I'll tell you . . . or, at least, I'll give you a hint.'

'Well?'

'It's a question I'm going to ask Superintendent Hennant. He knows the answer—you don't.'

'What question?'

'This one: Were Reg Tugwell's hands fastened in front of him or behind his back?'

'Which way will fit in with this daft idea of yours?'

Quinn said, 'Work it out for yourself. Meanwhile excuse me. I've got a very important phone call to make . . .'

CHAPTER XVII

SERGEANT FREESON took the call. He said, 'The superintendent's rather busy right now. Can I help you?'

With his eyes turned up to the ceiling, he listened. Then he grunted, 'I see. Hold on a moment.'

He put his hand over the mouthpiece, looked at Hennant and said, 'It's that crime reporter, sir—Quinn. He'd like to know if he can come and see you?'

'What does he want this time? I've nothing to add to the press release.'

'Yes, sir, but—'

'Tell him I heard all he had to say on Tuesday. He'd scarcely been gone an hour when he was on the phone again. I've had enough of his theories about Mrs Marshall's husband.'

'It isn't anything to do with that, sir. There's a question he'd like to ask you.'

'To do with what?'

'The patrolman at Jauncey's factory on the night the payroll was stolen, sir. Quinn wants to know how his hands were tied.'

The superintendent leaned back and plucked at his protruding lower lip while he stared with thoughtful eyes at the phone. He seemed in no hurry.

At last, he said, 'There's one thing, Sergeant, I'm prepared to admit. Whatever else Quinn may be he's certainly not a fool. Tell him I'll answer his question if he gets here before six o'clock.'

Quinn arrived at five minutes to six. It was windy and cold and the lights along the Embankment mirrored themselves in the fast-ebbing waters of the Thames like reflections from molten black glass.

Sergeant Freeson escorted him upstairs. '. . . The superintendent can't give you more than a few minutes, Mr Quinn. He has a conference with the Assistant Commissioner at six-fifteen.'

'A few minutes is all I need,' Quinn said.

He had begun to feel somewhat less sure of himself as he followed the sergeant along the corridor. It was a daft idea. Two and two never made five.

They stopped outside a door labelled: *PRIVATE*. Freeson tapped twice with his knuckles, gave Quinn a nod and told him to go in. '. . . I may see you before you leave.'

Superintendent Hennant was sitting behind his desk, arms folded, long legs outstretched. An open file lay on his blotting-pad.

He said, 'Come and sit down, Mr Quinn. I haven't much time to spare but I thought I'd better hear what you have to say. Experience has taught me you're a man with an original turn of mind.'

'That's putting it nicely,' Quinn said. 'Most people say I'm eccentric or ill-advised or just plain nicky.'

'You're joking, I know. However, what was this question you wanted to ask me?'

'It's about Reg Tugwell, the patrolman at Jauncey Engineering. You've heard, I suppose, that he's trying to fiddle some compensation for the injury he sustained on the night of the robbery?'

'Yes, I was told this afternoon he'd worked only one shift in the past week. Nothing's been seen of him since he came off duty nine o'clock Sunday morning. But how do you know it's a fiddle?'

'I had a chat with one of his mates last Sunday—a cynical character by the name of Alfie Platt. He's convinced Tugwell's putting on an act because he wasn't all that badly hurt.'

'What do you think?'

'I'm inclined to agree with Platt. Tugwell's recollection of events was just too detailed. For a man taken by surprise and knocked unconscious he remembers too much of what he'd seen.'

In a mild voice, Hennant asked, 'Are you afraid he'll obtain compensation by exaggerating his condition?'

Quinn said, 'No, I'm afraid of something a lot worse than that.'

'Something to do with the way his hands were tied?'

'Yes. It all depends on whether they were fastened together in front of him or behind his back.'

'And if I tell you they were tied in front?'

'Then, in my opinion, he might well have faked the whole thing,' Quinn said.

Hennant's sharp blue eyes narrowed. With no change of tone, he asked, 'Just what do you mean by that?'

'I think you know what I mean.'

'Do I?'

'Yes, of course you do. My journey wasn't really necessary, was it?'

A slow smile pulled up one side of Hennant's mouth. He said, 'Oh, I wouldn't say that. What you learned from Alfie Platt is quite useful. I'm glad to have the information. Anything you'd care to add to it?'

'No . . . but I'd like to ask another question, if you don't mind.'

'Not at all. Whatever we talk about, of course, is to be treated in the strictest confidence.'

'Of course. I was just wondering if you had any proof that Tugwell tied himself up.'

'So far—no. But it's only a few hours since the discovery of Graham's body switched our inquiries into an entirely new direction. For the time being we have to tread cautiously.'

'To bind and gag himself with adhesive plaster wouldn't have presented much of a problem,' Quinn said.

'Neither would the bump on his head—that's if he did the whole job by himself.'

'With an accomplice any fool could've done it.'

The smile touched Hennant's eyes. He said, 'Easier still with two accomplices.'

Quinn thought of the missing pieces that had been there all the time. He said, 'What I don't see is why Graham and his woman friend needed Reg Tugwell. They had the safe keys, the getaway vehicles and a snug hideout. Splitting the money two ways is better than three ways.'

The superintendent unfolded his arms and sat up and glanced at the open file on his desk. In a precise voice, he said, 'Tugwell may, or may not, have lied. Assuming he was involved in the theft there's one thing we know for certain: Mrs Marshall must've been in on it, too.'

'But not necessarily Graham. His prints would be on the glass paperweight because he often handled it. If he were victim instead of villain—'

'He'd be the one to get knocked over the head. The police doctor says he'd been struck with a lump of stone.'

'I didn't know that,' Quinn said.

'Well, actually there was nothing definite to show whether he'd been struck or landed on his head. A stone that could've caused the damage was found in the bottom of the trench.'

Hennant glanced at the file again. Then he went on, 'I've got proof he received the blow before he tumbled into the hole. On the assumption that he'd been attacked close to the Administration building I had a search made of the immediate area.'

'And you found the lump of rock that had been used,' Quinn said.

'Yes. Nothing clever in looking for something that common-sense tells you must be there.'

'Where was it?'

'Between the perimeter fence and the lawn in front of the Admin block. The distance would be a reasonable throw . . . assuming Graham was struck down while changing the spare wheel.'

'Find any other stones near the same spot?'

'Two or three.' Hennant's mouth twitched in another smile. 'You don't take anything for granted, do you?'

'Not after all the mare's nests I've been chasing,' Quinn said.

'Don't blame you. As it happens, I know this piece of rock is the one that was used. There were several hairs sticking to it—dark hairs with a hint of grey. The lab hasn't had time to compare them yet but I'll lay fair odds they're from Graham's head.'

'Which doesn't mean, of course, that he wasn't in it with Mrs Marshall and Tugwell.'

'If Tugwell did take part in the robbery. As you say, Graham and Yvonne Marshall didn't need him.'

'Maybe not. But if they cut him in for some reason we don't yet know, it could be he carried the elimination idea a stage further. No split at all meant he could keep the whole fifty-four thousand for himself.'

Hennant pulled at his lower lip. Then he said, 'That applies whether he was part of a team effort or merely gate-crashed. Perhaps he stumbled on the theft by sheer chance . . . just as he says.'

'But didn't get knocked out,' Quinn said. 'In return for a

share he promised to keep his mouth shut. Before he let her leave the factory he compelled Mrs Marshall to tell him where she intended to lie low with the money and—'

'—after she'd gone he eliminated Graham. Then there were two.'

'They often say—much wants more,' Quinn said. 'So poor little Yvonne got none.'

The superintendent closed the file on his desk and lay back and stretched. When he had looked at his watch, he said, 'It may be the logical explanation. Certainly accounts for what happened at Hilary Close.'

'Greed accounts for most villainy.'

'No, I don't think it was greed alone in this case. Getting rid of her served another purpose. Tugwell would never know what she might do if she found out he'd disposed of her lover. He couldn't be sure she wouldn't go screaming to the police.'

Quinn said, 'So all roads lead to Mister Reginald Tugwell. He had ample time to drive Graham's car to the dockside and abandon it there, returning to the works by taxi ... or a couple of minutes' walk from the factory.'

'And once back at Jauncey Engineering he banged his head to raise a nasty bruise and tied himself up with sticky tape. After that he had only to wait for the night patrolman to arrive at one a.m.'

'I should imagine he left the gates unlocked so he stood a chance of being discovered before then. Anyone who noticed they were unsecured would probably inform the police. That would save Tugwell having to lie on the floor bound hand and foot any longer than necessary.'

'But no one did notice,' Hennant said.

'Well, he couldn't expect to have everything his own way. He'd already had plenty of luck. Leaving the factory all that time was taking a pretty big risk: somebody might've discovered he'd gone.'

'True. But he was gambling for high stakes.'

Quinn looked at the clean shining ash-tray on the meticulously tidy desk. He asked, 'When you searched Graham's body did you find a key to the flat at Hilary Close?'

'No. If he'd ever had one it was taken from him before he was heaved into the trench and covered with some shovels of earth.'

The recollection of those moments when Mrs Wentworth rang the bell was clear in Quinn's mind. He told himself the whole story might never be revealed but that no longer mattered.

. . . Tugwell must've been in Flat 11 when I got to Hilary Close. He heard me coming up the stairs and waited until I'd gone into Mrs Wentworth's flat before he slipped out and tip-toed downstairs. He didn't close the door properly because he was afraid we'd hear the latch click . . .

Perhaps no one would ever know the truth about what happened at Jauncey Engineering that night. Perhaps Tugwell had unscrewed the valve of the tyre so that Graham would be left alone.

Only Tugwell knew what had driven him to kill— whether it was greed or some other motive. But the first murder had made the second one inevitable.

'So that's that,' Quinn said. 'We know who's got the payroll now . . . but I don't think much of your chances of getting Tugwell to tell you where he's hidden it.'

'I'll do my best,' Hennant said.

'What inducement can you offer him? If you can prove he killed both Graham and Mrs Marshall he'll get anything from, say, fourteen years down to nine or ten years. His sentence won't be any less if he discloses where he planted the cash. So why should he talk?'

Superintendent Hennant said, 'Go away before you depress me.'

'Better face the facts. If he keeps his mouth shut about the location of the money he may get away with double murder. If he talks he gets done—good and proper. One way he ends up with nothing. The other way he has fifty-four thousand quid waiting for him when he comes out.'

'If he lives to come out. Tugwell's in his middle fifties. Even fourteen years will bring him to close on seventy.'

'What difference can it make whatever he does? He won't

spend materially less time in gaol . . . assuming you're able to obtain a conviction. As I see it you've no hard evidence.'

'There are ways and means,' Hennant said.

'Not if he keeps on saying he don't know nothing. Supposing you don't get a conviction? He has only to stay away from the spot where he's planted the money and you're stumped. You can't keep him under surveillance for months, day in and day out, twenty-four hours a day.'

'Maybe not. But how long do you think it'll be before he gets an itchy palm?'

'Depends how clever he is. And he's been smart enough so far.'

Hennant nodded. He said, 'Yes, but so far it was all plain sailing. I'm fairly sure he thought Graham's body would never be found. The fact that we now know the cashier's dead is bound to worry Tugwell somewhat.'

'Providing he just goes on complaining about his headaches, he has nothing to worry about.'

'That's exactly what I want him to go on doing.' The superintendent leaned forward and stared into Quinn's face. 'He mustn't have the slightest idea we're waiting for him to make a wrong move.'

'You can't control the kind of ideas he gets,' Quinn said. 'Why are you looking at me like the Ancient Mariner?'

'I'll tell you why—but you mustn't take offence.'

'I can't take any more than you give,' Quinn said.

'All I want is to make the position clear.'

'OK. Make it.'

Superintendent Hennant sat back. In an even voice, he said, 'I only confided in you because you were already on the same track. Apart from the AC—and I haven't spoken to him yet—you and I will be the only people who'll know Tugwell's under suspicion.'

'Meaning what?'

'If he finds out—well, I don't need to dot the i's and cross the t's, do I?'

Quinn said, 'What you're saying is that I'm the only security risk.'

'No, Mr Quinn. I'm just trying to impress on you the necessity for extreme caution so that he has no chance to suspect.'

'I'm impressed,' Quinn said.

'Then I'll leave it there.'

'Good. Nice to know I'm trusted. All right if I change the subject?'

'Of course . . . but I haven't got much time. It's nearly a quarter past six.'

'This won't take long. Have you told Mrs Graham her husband's dead?'

'Not yet. It isn't the kind of job I relish.'

'Mind if I break the news to her before you do it formally?'

'No . . . I don't think so. But why should you want to do what most men shy away from?'

'I'm sorry for her,' Quinn said. 'We've met only once but she may take it better coming from me . . . especially if I get some moral support from her sister.'

'Never would've thought you were a sentimentalist, Mr Quinn.'

'Neither would I. Just feel in this case that Mrs Graham's been kicked around by all and sundry . . . including her late husband and his fancy woman.'

'Yes, I suppose you're right. Life hasn't been very kind to her.'

Hennant pushed himself to his feet. He asked, 'Will you be calling on the lady when you leave here?'

'If her sister can get away from the office,' Quinn said. 'I'd hate to be on my own with Mrs Graham if she threw a fit of hysterics.'

It was an evasion. He knew why he wanted Barbara to be there. They had known each other just a few days, but time was irrelevant. Those moments had given him a glimpse of a new existence.

Harold Graham had brought them together. But while he lived, Harold Graham would have kept them apart. Now he was dead. Now the barrier had gone.

As though listening to the voice of someone else, Quinn

could hear himself saying, '... *After this is all over and done with do you think we might meet somewhere one night . . .?*'

No one could have anticipated how soon his hopes would be realized. It was all over.

... Hard lines on Ethel Graham but Barbara doesn't have to go into mourning. She hasn't suffered any bereavement. And if Ethel faces up to the situation she must recognize she's better off. She's still young enough to start a new life, to stand on her own feet instead of leaning on Barbara ...

Then he had said good night to Hennant and he was outside on the wind-swept Embankment with his raincoat flapping against his legs. He feld cold and hungry. It had been a long time since his usual scratch lunch. Before he even considered going out to Crouch End he must have something to eat.

From a phone box that reeked of stale tobacco-smoke he rang Barbara's office. While he listened to the *burr-burr ... burr-burr ... burr-burr* at the other end of the line he asked himself what he should say, how much he could reveal without breaking trust with Superintendent Hennant. It made no difference to her or her sister how Harold Graham had died. Whatever his sins they would be buried with him.

Tugwell ... or a man called Marshall ... it was unimportant now. It had been unimportant from the very start.

If Graham had lived to get away with Jauncey's payroll his wife would never have seen him again. To her he would have been as good as dead ... with the added bitterness that he had betrayed her for another woman. She was better off this way. In time she would come to realize that.

There the phone clicked and he heard Barbara's voice. It gave him the old heady sensation like the effect of drink on an empty stomach.

He took a deep breath and asked, 'Are you likely to be visiting your sister tonight?'

Barbara said, 'Oh, it's you! Strange I should be thinking about you only a little while ago.'

'If you didn't feel it was strange I'd be flattered,' Quinn said.

'Oh, I didn't mean it like that. I was wondering if your cold was better.'

'How did you know I had a cold?'

'Well, you were coughing quite a lot the other night.'

'I'm always coughing.'

'That's silly. You should take something for it.'

'Sounds like the feed line in a Xmas cracker joke,' Quinn said. 'But thanks for being concerned about me. I don't come across it very often.'

'Perhaps you don't give people a chance.'

'What is it I do to stop them?'

'You go around feeling sorry for yourself . . . don't you?'

'Maybe. But I didn't know it showed.'

In a humble voice, Barbara said, 'Now I've offended you. It was wrong of me to talk like that. Please forgive me.'

'There's nothing to forgive. Somebody ought to have said it long ago. If you want the truth, I'm grateful.'

'Do you really mean that?'

'I wouldn't say it if I didn't. Now can I ask you again if you'll be seeing your sister tonight?'

'Well, I hadn't intended to. Was there something you wanted me to tell her?'

Quinn said, 'No, I've got something to discuss with her and I'd like you to be there.'

'No reason why I can't be.'

'Good. I'll see you later.'

She made a little sound of protest. Then she asked hesitantly, 'Was—was that all? Aren't you going to tell me what's wrong?'

'Nothing's wrong—nothing that need affect you and me. I have some information for Mrs Graham that I thought you'd want to hear.'

'About Harold?'

'Yes, it has to do with your brother-in-law.'

'In that case—' there was a tremble in Barbara's voice— 'it can't be good news.'

'Depends on how you look at it,' Quinn said.

CHAPTER XVIII

HE ATE WITH ONE HAND while he typed out his story with the other—the story of a man who had been lying dead in a flooded trench ever since the night when the Jauncey payroll theft took place. Now the police hunt would switch direction.

But after a whole week the scent was cold. Motives had changed and there were no descriptions to follow. The task of the police had become infinitely more difficult. Their problem was where to begin.

Two people had reached out for a stolen fortune—two people blinded by visions of wealth and a romantic life together. They had no way of knowing it was death they released when they opened the safe at Jauncey Engineering.

He drank a second cup of tea while he read through his finished copy. It was a good story. He had to admit it himself. All the right ingredients were there—sex, robbery, betrayal and murder. And a new puzzle had replaced the old one. That added extra spice. The public would lap it up.

Quinn wondered how many people would think of a man called Marshall or the widow of Harold Graham. They were just two pieces of flotsam cast up by the tide of events.

It was unlikely they would ever meet. The inquest on Graham and the adjourned inquest on Yvonne Marshall would be held at different times. Nothing now linked widow and widower.

. . . Funny how people alter. Graham must've been in love with Ethel when he was asked: Wilt thou have this woman to thy wedded wife . . .? Nobody will ever know when his feelings towards her changed . . .

There must have come a time when he no longer wanted to live with her. Perhaps it would never have happened if he had not become infatuated with Yvonne Marshall.

He was the right age. Infatuation or real love—the end result was the same.

Men in the grip of the same primitive urge had been known to get rid of their wives. Harold Graham was more civilized. He had found a way of escape without recourse to murder.

... Forsaking all other, keep thee only unto her, so long as ye both shall live ...

Graham had never guessed his life would be forfeit. Ethel had gained her freedom—unsought and unwanted. His escape had been death in a waterlogged trench.

Strange how things worked out. A man and his mistress had planned to run away together ... and now they were together. Perhaps in the beginning fate had decided that they belonged to each other.

Quinn told himself he was getting soft in the head. Life followed no rigid pattern. Destiny had more to do than shape the lives of petty individuals.

Yet he was thinking of Barbara as he came out into the raw cold of Fleet Street and set off to walk to Holborn underground. If she had not been at the house in Maryland Avenue that day they first met ... if Harold Graham had not planned to rob his employers ... if ... if ... step by step backwards into the past.

... You're kidding yourself if you imagine she's serious. Just because she's been nice to you doesn't mean she'd have you as a husband. Takes two to make a bargain. And let's face it, mate, you're no bargain for a girl like Barbara Field ...

Alternate hope and dejection kept him company on his way to Crouch End. As he came out of the station he was tempted to phone her and make some excuse. The police could tell Mrs Graham her husband was dead. It was their job.

If Barbara got to know how he felt she would laugh at him. He could take anything but that ... anything but ridicule. His best plan would be to find a nice cosy pub and drink beer until he had given Superintendent Hennant time to convey the news personally to Mrs Graham.

Yet it would serve no purpose to dodge the issue. He had to know. Sooner or later he had to know. Better now . . . better now . . . better now . . . The words kept time with his footsteps as he approached No. 14 Maryland Avenue, his head bent to the wind, his hands bunched in his raincoat pockets.

He ran a comb through his hair when he had rung the bell. No sense in letting Barbara think he was something that had escaped from a student demo. His chances were poor enough already.

Then the light came on in the hall. He had barely time to get rid of his comb before the door opened.

Barbara was glad to see him. It showed in her smile and the light of welcome that came into her warm brown eyes. He had never seen anyone look at him as she was looking at him now.

When she had invited him in and closed the door, she said, 'There's been a phone call for you. Not two minutes ago. Superintendent Hennant wanted to know if we'd seen you. I told him you hadn't arrived yet but we expected you very soon.'

'Does he want me to ring him back?'

'No. It didn't seem to be anything important. But if you'd like to have a word with him . . .'

Quinn said, 'After I've spoken to your sister. Did you tell her I was coming?'

'Yes. You didn't say I shouldn't . . . and I had to explain what I was doing here.'

'Of course. Don't worry about it.'

He was thinking of a night, eight days ago, when two people had rifled the safe at Jauncey Engineering and a man called Tugwell had been found trussed up with adhesive plaster. So two people became three . . . and Mick Pavitt, the sneak-thief, made four . . . and Keith Marshall was five.

Like the ripples on a pond when someone tosses a stone

from the bank. The stone disappears but the ripples spread out in ever-widening circles until they can no longer be seen.

... But before the energy of that stone is spent they engulf each tiny object in their path. Everything they touch is moved on to a different course. Nothing can ever be quite the same again ...

It was a stone that had ended Graham's dreams of a new life. Then the ripples sent Yvonne to her death. Now they were lapping against Reg Tugwell.

Barbara asked, 'Are you cross with me?'

Her eyes were subdued but her smile was still very sweet. He remembered a saying: *Out of evil cometh good.* Now he knew what it meant. She made everything worth while.

He said, 'No, not in the least. My mind was a long way off . . . that's all.'

She nodded as though she understood. Then she led him into the room where her sister was waiting.

Mrs Graham seemed to have become more relaxed in the past forty-eight hours. He told himself there was a limit to what a woman could endure. When that limit was reached she had to learn to accept. It was calm acceptance that he saw in Ethel Graham's small placid face.

Quinn told her she had been right in thinking her husband had not caused the death of Yvonne Marshall. There was now proof that it must have been someone else.

'. . . I thought you might prefer to hear it from me.'

'That was very considerate of you. When did you get to know?'

'Late this afternoon.'

Her dark eyes studied him for a long moment. Then she said, 'If that was all you had to tell me you'd have phoned. So there must be something more.'

Quinn said, 'There is. It'll be in tomorrow's papers. By that time the police will have been in touch with you.'

'But—' her eyes clung to his face while she wrapped one hand in the other and squeezed tightly—'but you wanted to break the news more gently. Is that why you came?'

'Yes'

'You're very kind.'

In a voice little more than a whisper, she repeated, 'Very kind.'

He waited. Barbara was watching her sister as though from a distance. He told himself that Barbara knew.

Mrs Graham said, 'This news you've brought can't be that my husband's been arrested. You wouldn't have talked about proof . . . unless he couldn't have murdered that woman Marshall. And they're sure he didn't do it, aren't they?'

'Beyond any shadow of doubt,' Quinn said.

'That can mean—' she swallowed with difficulty—'that can mean only one thing. You've come to tell me he's—he's dead.'

Quinn nodded. Now it was over. Now he could leave Ethel Graham to find peace within herself. He owed no duty to her. She might be Barbara's sister but she had to bear her own cross. Someday he would see her again. Someday . . .

From where she stood beside the window, Barbara asked in a husky voice, 'How did it happen?'

'He was found half-buried on a building site at the factory. According to the police doctor he must've been there since the night of the robbery.'

Ethel Graham sat twisting her hands together, over and over again, while she stared into the barren distance. There was no grief in her eyes.

At last, she said, 'If that woman Marshall hadn't died, too, I could almost have believed she'd killed Harold so as to have all the money herself.'

Quinn said, 'So could I. But now it's obvious that both of them were murdered by a third party.'

Very faintly, Mrs Graham asked, 'In the same way?'

'No. If it's any consolation to you he didn't suffer. The doctor says he died from drowning. The trench he was buried in had two or three feet of water in it.'

She sat trembling, the ghosts of terrible things in her eyes. After a long silence, she said, 'Do they know how he came to be there?'

'Well, the indications are that he was struck on the head and then dragged or carried to the place where a new building is being erected. The police believe that whoever did it thought your husband's body would remain hidden until the trench was filled in after all the work was completed.'

'If he hadn't been found, people would've thought he'd killed that woman Marshall.' Mrs Graham moistened her pale lips. 'They're bound to have thought that.'

'And they'd have gone on thinking it,' Quinn said.

'Because—' her mouth was a thin hard line—'because they were meant to. Right from the start, the one who did it intended my husband to take the blame. Anybody like that can have no human feelings.'

In a flat voice, Barbara said, 'Only hate. That's all.'

'If you're referring to Keith Marshall, you're wrong,' Quinn said. 'It's most unlikely he had anything to do with it.'

'Why do you say that? What's made you change your mind since Tuesday night?'

'Circumstances changed it for me. The only thing I'm sure of now is that the same person killed both of them.'

'Yes, of course. Once he'd got rid of Harold, he had to see she didn't talk. If ever Harold's body was found she'd have guessed the truth . . .'

Quinn knew it was time he left. If he stayed any longer he might betray Hennant's confidence.

'. . . She'd know it had happened when he was changing the wheel after she'd gone,' Barbara said. 'And there was only one person who could have found out what they'd planned to do that night.'

'I thought so, too, until this afternoon,' Quinn said.

'And now you know it wasn't her husband?'

'Well, I wouldn't exactly say that. In fact, I'm not supposed to discuss it at all. So if you don't mind . . .'

'No . . . no, of course not.' Barbara tried to smile. 'I'm sorry if I've embarrassed you. It wasn't fair.'

'Don't apologize,' Quinn said. 'I realize the effect all this has had on you and your sister. Nasty business. Coming right out of the blue makes it so much worse.'

He was hiding his thoughts behind a stream of words that ran on beyond his control. There were other things he wanted to say—things for Barbara alone to hear.

But that would come later when they met outside this house where the atmosphere was poisoned with black memories of the days leading up to Harold Graham's death. In time his widow would cleanse the place with fresh air and sunlight. In time . . .

Quinn wondered why Hennant had phoned. Perhaps it was only to find out whether Mrs Graham had been told of their discovery. The superintendent would have to notify her officially but his task would be far less unpleasant now that somebody else had broken the news.

Like a muffled radio inside his head, Quinn could hear a voice saying, '. . . *This is the news . . . the news . . . the news.*'

A radio had been playing in the flat occupied by the woman who called herself Mrs Cooke. He remembered he had switched it off and how silence closed in around him as though it had been kept at bay only by the muted sound of music.

Other voices thrust themselves into his pattern of recollections, louder and louder, until there was no room for coherent thought. When at last the noise was stilled, just one voice remained.

'. . . *The news . . . the news . . . the news . . .*' It went on and on in mad repetition, without meaning, without any kind of sense.

Mrs Graham seemed to be listening to that same recurring voice, her small face dejected, her eyes remote as though fixed on something far off in space and time. She was no longer part of the lonely house in Maryland Avenue.

At the back of Quinn's mind two names were printed in burning letters—Tugwell and Marshall. One of them had been at the factory that night, the other could have been there. One of them could have crept up on a man who was stooped over the rear wheel of his car. With the rain beating down on him he would have heard nothing.

Already the level of water must have been rising in the

trench that was to be his grave. Already death was poised to strike him down. When the last wheel-nut had been tightened his last moment would have arrived . . .

Then Quinn knew. Beyond question, beyond all doubt, he knew.

Someone else would have to seek out the proof but it should not be hard to find. After that the machine would be set in motion. When it stopped, the world for many people would be a different place.

He fought against the shock of revelation that froze all his reflexes. Like a man in a dream he was pinned to the spot where he stood. He wanted to get away, to run and go on running until he had forgotten the house in Maryland Avenue where Harold Graham's widow grieved over the broken fragments of her marriage.

But this was no dream. This was a nightmare from which he would never awake. This was the most terrible moment of his whole life.

Ethel Graham watched him as he stood up. She asked, 'What's wrong? Why are you looking at me like that?'

'Because I'm sorry for you,' Quinn said. 'I wish to God I'd never come here tonight. I should've told Superintendent Hennant to do his own dirty work.'

'What on earth are you talking about? I thought it was most kind of you—'

'Blind is the right word—not kind. They say the road to hell is paved with good intentions . . . and my only excuse is that I meant well. If I hadn't been a blind fool I'd have minded my own business.'

He felt sick at his thoughts but he had to go on. In a voice he barely recognized as his own, he asked, 'Did you know your husband's car had a flat tyre the night all this began?'

She pressed her small slim hands together and put them to her mouth while she pondered. Then she said, 'No . . . no, I don't think you mentioned it.'

'That's right,' Quinn said. 'I didn't.'

Now he had arrived at the moment of truth. And he had to go on. The road back was impassable.

Barbara had a bewildered look in her eyes. She stared at

him as though she had never seen him before when he pivoted to face her squarely.

He said, 'But you knew about it. You knew your brother-in-law was struck down while he was changing the spare wheel. How did you happen to know?'

Fear drove bewilderment from her eyes. She said huskily, 'I read about it in one of the papers. I can't remember which one but—'

'Don't bother to try. It never appeared in any paper. Until this afternoon the police couldn't be sure the wheel was changed when the car was inside the factory grounds or somewhere else.'

'So you're calling me a liar. Is that it?'

Suddenly she looked different. Her mouth was no longer sweet, her face was pinched and cold.

'That's exactly it,' Quinn said. 'I'm calling you a liar—and worse.'

He wanted to hate her for what she had done but he could feel neither hatred nor regret. His emotions were a dried-up husk blown to and fro by the wind of contempt.

Mainly the contempt was for himself. All along she had led him by the nose. But for that he would have told her to say nothing. If he kept his mouth shut, too, she might well go free.

In a thin voice, she said, 'I don't understand what's come over you. All at once you've changed.'

'Neither of us has changed. We're just seeing each other as we've always been. I'm a damn fool—and you're the killer who murdered your brother-in-law and his mistress.'

Mrs Graham made a harsh sound of protest. She said, 'No ... no, it isn't true. I'll never believe it ... never ... never ... never!'

She was talking to Quinn but looking at her sister. And that look told him her denials meant no more than the crying of a child in the dark.

Barbara had nothing left to say. She was stricken with something greater than fear, something which locked body and mind so that she seemed unable to move.

In a wailing voice, Ethel went on '... You were in love

with Harold. He never realized how you felt about him although I've always known it. But you couldn't have done what this man says you did. You just couldn't. Whatever Harold may have been . . .'

For a long time no one spoke. Then Barbara said without any trace of emotion, 'You're a fool. All your life you've been a fool. For months you've known what was going on but you shut your eyes to it. So far as you were concerned he could do no wrong.'

Ethel turned her head stiffly and looked at Quinn. She said, 'I loved my husband. Whatever he did I was equally responsible . . . because I failed him. But my sister didn't understand. I should never have told her it worried me when he began coming home late.'

'You weren't to know how it would end,' Quinn said.

'But I shouldn't have talked about him. She thought what she was doing was for my sake. You must see that. It's all my fault. If you judge her you must also judge me.'

'I've no right to judge anybody,' Quinn said.

Barbara took a hesitant step towards him. With the faintest thread of hope running through her voice, she asked, 'Do you have to tell the police?'

There was an unspoken promise behind the words. As a bribe for his silence she was offering not only money—more money than he had ever possessed—but also herself.

He said, 'I have no choice. You can't pay me to become an accessory to murder.'

'It needn't be—' she came still closer—'like that at all. What we do afterwards is between you and me. Just forget you came here tonight. No one will ever know. It'll be our secret.'

While the moment of temptation lasted he was afraid he might yield. It was all so very simple. He had only to say nothing, to behave as though it had never happened. So very simple . . .

Then the thought of what her promise meant filled him with revulsion. She would destroy him as she had destroyed herself.

Now he must complete the final degradation. He had no other way out.

In all innocence he had stumbled on the truth—the innocence of a romantic idiot. It did no good to tell himself he had had a lucky escape. That was stupid self-deception. He had escaped nothing. The price would have to be paid.

He wondered whether it was wounded vanity or loss of self-respect that hurt him more. The only saving grace was that people were unlikely to find out how far he had been led by a girl with shining hair and wistful brown eyes . . .

Ethel Graham was looking at him. Ethel Graham was saying, '. . . My sister is wrong, Mr Quinn. It doesn't matter what you do. I'll know—and I'll tell.'

Barbara said hurriedly, 'You wouldn't. You don't really mean that. I did it all for you. He deserted you for that woman Marshall and he didn't care—'

'But I cared,' Ethel said. 'I still care. I was his wife.'

'An unwanted wife. Can't you get it into your head that he left you for another woman?'

'Perhaps he did. That's none of your business. In any case you're no better than she was. You'd have stolen him from me if you'd had the chance. But he didn't want you. So you decided you'd have the money instead.'

She turned to Quinn and asked, 'What are you going to do?'

Barbara Field had gone very still. Her eyes became empty and desolate when Quinn said, 'Exactly what I meant to do all along. I'm phoning Superintendent Hennant.'

CHAPTER XIX

PIPER FOUND HIM in the lounge of the Three Feathers. He was parked on a stool in his usual corner of the horseshoe bar, his face subdued, one hand propping up his chin. In front of him stood a half-empty pint glass.

'I thought somehow I'd find you here,' Piper said. 'Didn't you get my message?'

Quinn sat up and pushed back a strand of lank hair. Without much enthusiasm, he said, 'Oh, hullo. Nice to see you. What'll you have?'

'An answer to my question will do to start with,' Piper said.

'Question? What question?' He rapped on the bar. 'Freddie! There's a cash customer here who wants a bit of service.'

The weasel-faced barman limped towards them, his eyes wide in mock astonishment. He said, 'It speaks. Heaven be praised, it speaks. At long last the spell is broken.'

He put his open hands together and bowed low and asked, 'What is your will, O, Master?'

Quinn said, 'Comics . . . the world's full of comics. Fetch my friend a large whisky and add a half of bitter to my glass. Might put some life in it.'

'Take more than that to put some life in you,' Freddie said.

He served them and went away. Piper said, 'I don't often have double whiskies during business hours. What are we celebrating?'

'Celebrating?' Quinn looked at him vaguely. 'Does it have to be a celebration before I can buy you a decent drink?'

'No, but it's never happened before. Must be a special occasion.'

'Well, yes—' there was a strange look in Quinn's eyes— 'you might say that.'

'So?'

'So nothing. That's all.'

Piper said, 'Before this gets completely beyond me let's start again. I phoned your office this morning and left a message asking you to ring me back. Didn't anyone tell you?'

'Oh, yes, they told me all right. I was going to give you a buzz later.'

'When later?'

'Soon's I got things straightened out.'

'Is that what you're doing here?'

'More or less.'

'You don't seem to have done much straightening. If you're in some kind of trouble can I help?'

Quinn said, 'Thanks, but it's nothing like that. I was damn near in trouble, as it happens, but I'm not now.'

'What does that mean? Of course, if you'd rather not talk about it . . .'

'Oh, I don't mind. Maybe better for me if I get it off my chest.'

He swallowed a mouthful of bitter. Then he asked, 'You've heard the outcome of the Jauncey payroll case?'

'Yes, I read your column in this morning's paper,' Piper said. 'Seems we were 'way off the track. Where did Superintendent Hennant get his bright idea?'

With a sour look in his eyes, Quinn said, 'From me. But I don't want you to think there was anything clever about it. I just happened to be around at the time. All I did was make a phone call . . .'

Piper listened as Piper always listened. When he had heard the whole story, he said, 'Doesn't matter how the truth came out. You're entitled to claim the reward.'

Quinn took a long slow drink. When he put his glass down he shrugged and said, 'There isn't any reward. She refuses to say where she hid the money. In fact, she denies the whole thing. If she has the right counsel to defend her, I wouldn't be at all surprised . . .' He shrugged again.

'But Hennant must be pretty sure he's got a case,' Piper said.

'Naturally. Among other things, the police have analysed mud from the floor of her car and they can prove it came from the building site at the factory.'

'How does she explain that?'

'Says she picked up Graham one night and it must've come off his shoes.'

'And he's the only one who could've proved she's lying,' Piper said.

'Exactly. They've also got hold of a witness who saw

her snooping near the Marshalls' house in Dollis Hill a couple of times. It was dark on both occasions and I wouldn't gamble on how the witness will stand up to cross-examination.'

'Anything else?'

'Yes. Somebody who lives in Molineux Crescent—that's a street near Jauncey's factory—says he saw a car parked there on the night of the robbery. He's confident the registration number was the same as her Triumph Convertible.'

'How long was it there?'

'Several hours . . . from about half-past four until long after eight o'clock. Up to five o'clock anybody can get into the factory if they say they've come on business. Hennant thinks she hid in one of the toilets until all the staff had gone home . . .'

It fitted neatly, Piper told himself. Graham bound and gagged the patrolman and took his Security Office key so as to obtain the key to Bransby Lane gates.

. . . He relocked the Security door, opened the gates and let Yvonne Marshall out. When she left he probably relocked the gates so that passers-by wouldn't suspect anything was wrong. The odds are he intended to do the same thing when he left . . .

But Graham had not lived to do so. And his killer was in too great a hurry to get away.

Piper said, 'She drove Graham's car to the docks, took a taxi back to Molineux Crescent and then went home. There was no rush to carry out stage two: she knew where the payroll had been taken. For weeks she must've kept watch on Graham—'

'—and listened-in to what went on between his lady-love and himself,' Quinn said. 'Just one thing puzzles me. If Tugwell hadn't poked his nose in where it wasn't wanted and if he hadn't been knocked over the head, he wouldn't have opened the gates to let anybody but a member of the staff leave. So how would she have got out?'

'One person could tell you,' Piper said. 'But she won't.'

Once again Quinn remembered the hurt he had felt. It spoiled the taste of his beer.

He said, 'I wouldn't believe her even if she did. I've lost my faith in human nature.'

'Didn't know you had any.'

'Well, I did. But she knocked it out of me.'

'All women aren't the same,' Piper said.

'How do you know the good from the bad before it's too late?'

'Usually by instinct.'

'Is that so? Well, my instinct stinks.'

'We all make mistakes.'

'So they say. I'm such a clever boy I went and made two.'

Over the rim of his glass, Quinn added, 'Stupid ones. Remember I told you a nice girl wouldn't have me?'

'Yes.'

'Well, my second mistake was in thinking she fancied me at all.'

'And your first one?'

'That she was a nice girl,' Quinn said. 'I should be locked up for my own protection.'

He emptied his glass and thumped it on the bar. Freddie looked round and asked, 'Is that the royal summons I hear ... or has this place been turned into a knocking shop?'

Piper said, 'My friend will have the same again, please.'

'And you, sir?'

'Nothing for me. But take one for yourself.'

'Thank you, sir. It's a pleasure to deal with a gentleman —for a change.'

He stood a pint of bitter in front of Quinn and left them. From the other end of the bar, he called out, 'Your good health, sir. I hope your generosity is infectious ... present company included.'

Quinn took a slow thoughtful drink and smacked his lips. He said, 'At least, the beer's constant.'

Then he looked at Piper. With a sudden grin, he asked, 'Ever feel it's all for the best?'

'Acceptance is the beginning of wisdom,' Piper said.

'Ah, very profound. So you also believe there is a destiny that shapes our ends, rough-hew them how we will?'

'Divinity,' Piper said. 'Not destiny.'

'You don't say?'

'No, I don't. But Hamlet did. You should check your Shakespeare.'

Quinn said, 'Why should I bother when you're around? And you know what?'

'Well?'

'I've got a funny feeling it didn't happen to me but to someone else.'

'Good. I don't like to see you looking miserable.'

'Me? Miserable?'

He savoured another mouthful of bitter. As he put down his glass, he said, 'It's a long road that hasn't got a silver lining just before the dawn . . . if I may coin a phrase. Good job things didn't work out differently, taken all round.'

'Why?'

'I'd have had to buy a new raincoat,' Quinn said.